CHAMELEON IN A CANDY STORE

ANONYMOUS

CHAMELEON IN A CANDY STORE

ANONYMOUS

CHAMELEON IN A CANDY STORE
ANONYMOUS

GALLERY BOOKS

New York London Toronto Sydney New Delhi

G

Gallery Books
An Imprint of Simon & Schuster, Inc.
1230 Avenue of the Americas
New York, NY 10020

This title was previously published as *Chameleon on a Kaleidoscope*.

First Gallery Books trade paperback edition March 2017

GALLERY BOOKS and colophon are registered trademarks of
Simon & Schuster, Inc.

For information about special discounts for bulk purchases,
please contact Simon & Schuster Special Sales at 1-866-506-1949
or business@simonandschuster.com.

The Simon & Schuster Speakers Bureau can bring authors
to your live event. For more information or to book an event
contact the Simon & Schuster Speakers Bureau at 1-866-248-3049
or visit our website at www.simonspeakers.com.

Manufactured in the United States of America

10   9   8   7   6   5   4

Library of Congress Cataloging-in-Publication Data is available.

ISBN 978-1-5011-6979-3
ISBN 978-1-5011-7005-8 (ebook)

CHAMELEON IN A CANDY STORE
ANONYMOUS

CHAMELEON IN A CANDY STORE

ANONYMOUS

1

I knew if I wanted to have sex with a girl within the first three seconds of meeting her.

After that, it was just a matter of how much I was willing to put up with to make it happen. This period of putting up with their bullshit was what women called charm.

On dates with girls I didn't even like trying to get into pants that didn't even fit.

Rummaging around inside them looking for what? Had this always been the case even before the drinking? If so, all I'd done was exchange one addiction for another. Far from being free, the prison had just gotten bigger. And they just sat there, protected by the romantic rules of engagement, categorizing my attempts at fucking them. How did I compare to the guy last night? At least he paid for dinner. And wanted children. He was taller too. I was happy to let the gargoyle in my midriff drag me to within fucking distance of these creatures, but even I couldn't make myself pretend I wanted babies.

YVETTE

Bobbing and swaying in front of my face as we ascended the steps to her fourth-floor Elizabeth Street apartment was the real reason we'd been together three years. Our evening stroll had been cut short by a rainstorm, so once we got inside we shook off our wet things. We lay across her bed and chatted. Ordinarily this would have been enough to get the ball rolling, but I was still not confident about making a move. I had already discovered that working for a bad ad agency required just as much energy as working for a good one, and I had an early start the next day. If we didn't have sex soon I'd be forced to stay the entire night. Did she want me to leave? Time to call her bluff. Making an overly dramatic announcement that I had better go if I was to be in decent shape for work the next day, I began to say my good-byes to that magnificent world-class ass.

"You hug it like it's a separate person," she said, thawing a little.

"You're accusing me of having an affair with your ass, behind your back?"

2

A smile.

She was pissed because I hadn't picked up on her latest hint that we should live together, get married, have children, and die of old age in each other's arms. These hints had more recently taken the form of exaggerated street mimes. The huge overacted crazy-eyed smile she reserved for babies was subtle compared to the impossible affection conjured up in the presence of every old couple we encountered. Especially, for some reason, if they were Asian. I resisted the urge to respond or acknowledge because I knew that once the subject was brought out into the open, it could never be put back in the box. There was no way I was going to marry her, but there was no way I'd be allowed access to her ass if she knew this. I hoped that my silence would indicate that I was still open to the possibilities, but it was only a matter of time before something would need to be said.

I felt sufficiently encouraged by that halfhearted smile to spank her gently through her cotton knickers. This led to touching and tickling, pecking and pouting, and after she broke away to brush her teeth, turn out the lights, and close her laptop, we progressed to sensual half-lit sex. She fluttered up and down on me with such delicacy I was reminded of a winged nymph as she effortlessly hovered and dipped.

The rain persisted outside, and as she leaned back to scratch gently under my balls, I got a perfect view of her small dancer's breasts, backlit by the amber glow from the desk lamp. I stiffened inside her and her body immediately straightened as if we really had become one.

I wanted to say *I love you,* but it was too risky. She would surely see through it for the manipulation it was and stop what she was doing. I toyed with saying *You're lovely,* but this just felt childish. *I adore you* was merely *I love you* lite, and *oh baby* was completely meaningless.

"Fuck yeah," I said at last.

Well, at least it was honest.

Through a monthly showreel called *Shotz,* I found out that a copywriter I'd worked with at my former ad agency had since become a director of commercials. He was mentioned in the New Directors section, and nestled among the self-conscious up-to-the-minute motion graphics was a link to his finished commercial, which if it was a piece of shit would have been fine, but it wasn't. It was actually quite good. And the reason is was quite good was because it was my idea. He and I had talked about making the same commercial for our client BNV when we were at Killallon Fitzpatrick, but for some reason it never got presented, I think because it was thought to be too British for the American market. And now to add disgust to discomfort, I saw that this commercial was for Olaffson.

Olaffson was my account at my new agency.

Was this his way of getting back at me for leaving him in the freezing wastes of Saint Lacroix? I thought I was being paranoid until I saw the casting. The guy in the commercial looked pretty much like me. He knew I worked on Olaffson. The whole situation was weird because it wasn't even a real ad. It was a spec commercial, the kind of thing a new director puts on his reel to show he can make a theoretical concept work in thirty seconds. And anyway he hadn't succeeded in making it work; this concept—*my* concept—was much better suited to BNV because Olaffson made safe boring cars as opposed to flashy luxurious ones. He'd shot the ad exactly as we had discussed it, like a pastiche of a British public service announcement.

It opened with a title.

The Beginner's Guide to Lip-Reading
A young woman looks earnestly into the camera.
"Bastard," she says.
"Bastard," she says again.
Cut to an extreme close-up of her mouth as she pronounces the word soundlessly now so we can recognize it when spoken.
"Bastard." She mouths it again.
Cut to a street scene in which a young trendy man, looking suspiciously like Erik, strolls confidently up to a new Olaffson and jabs his electronic key at the sleek crouched vehicle before opening the door, disappearing inside it. On the other side of the street a pale young man with a shaved head, looking suspiciously like me,

5

watches the car drive smoothly away just as we see him say
something. It's a two-syllable word. A title appears across
the bottom of the screen. Outruns Green-Eyed Monsters:
Olaffson

I casually mentioned to Yvette that it might be a relief to
get out of advertising.

"How are you going to bring up kids if you haven't got
a good job?"

There was no way to answer this truthfully without
robbing myself of sex, and so, attempting to redirect the
subject, I told her I wanted to go back to London and write
a book in my newly paid-off flat. It had been her idea that
I pay off the mortgage on my London flat so that the rent
received from tenants could be treated as salary. With no
rent or mortgage hanging over me, I could always go on the
dole for pocket money.

"A man who goes on welfare by choice is a disgrace."

Obviously her vision of my future involved me working my ass off to keep her in expensive clothes, which she'd
wear to fancy dinners I was ostensibly going to treat her to.
Her reaction confirmed what I was already thinking: That I
should never tell her what I was thinking.

My continued presence would be understood as an
agreement to marry, and there was no way that was ever
going to happen. Up to that point I had feigned interest in
whatever she pointed me toward, as long as I was sexually

rewarded. And the sex was so influential I had managed to convince myself I wasn't even acting. I was more than happy to pay for the restaurants, the Broadway plays, and even the jewelry she picked out as long as we continued with our unspoken agreement that I would be sexually compensated. And for the first year we had been very fair about this distribution of sexual currency.

Her first. Then me.

But more recently, a new worrying pattern had begun to emerge where my orgasm couldn't even be contemplated until she had come not just once, but twice.

It was starting to feel like my second high-stress job. And it wasn't as if she was scorching hot. Yes, her body was fabulous, and yes, she was French (that accent alone got me hard), but her face was far from perfect, and I could hardly admit it to myself but she had some sort of skin problem where hardheaded yellowy protrusions would periodically emerge without warning. Why did I have to settle for that? I was living in New York, where I regularly encountered four or five life-changing women on the way to the subway.

When we first met I was still reeling from a romantic catastrophe that would eventually become the subject of my first book, so I wasn't even remotely looking for a girlfriend. But Yvette knew what it was to be foreign in the United States, and this was something that immediately drew us together. In fact, we were thrown together. An account man from the agency I worked for hosted a rooftop party for some Olaffson clients and I had to attend. Yvette seemed unaccustomed to social situations and I was not exactly an old hand myself, but like all Europeans, we enjoyed the luxury of being able to encapsulate the world's problems in one word.

"Americans."

We rolled our eyes knowingly.

It was obvious even in her staid work clothes that there was a great body under there, but I honestly didn't see her as a sexual possibility until months later. The fact that she was French was something I couldn't ignore. She loved toilet humor. Anything to do with piss or poop and she began to giggle like a sneaky schoolgirl at the back of the class. Her pet name for me was poopie-head. She sometimes even repeated the word during sex: "*Poopie, poopie.*"

Freud would have a field day.

She loved to show me the contents of her mouth while she ate. Especially in expensive restaurants. She'd beckon me toward her as if she had a secret to share, her hand shielding her mouth from the rest of the restaurant, and at the last moment she'd open her mouth wide, revealing mashed bouillabaisse and bread. When I appeared sufficiently disgusted, her hand morphed from horror-shield to giggle-guard and she sat back into her chair, satisfied.

She was impossible to sleep beside. I'd lie motionless at three-thirty in her moonlit bedroom, her arm heavy as a fallen beam across my chest, afraid to move for fear of waking her up and accidentally initiating a wee-hours discussion about how distant I was. Did I feel I was distant? Why was I always so distant?

"Distant? What? Yvette, I'm right here."

Then fondling my balls, she'd whisper, "You're not nice with me," and I'd find myself inside her. How ridiculously easy it is to get inside a vagina when the owner actually wants you in it. And as her weightless silhouette gyrated above me I knew better than to come. That was the ultimate act of selfishness.

Not yet fully awake, she is moving like an animal silent and sure, her palms pressed flat on my chest so that her groin insists itself against me, scratching some unbearable, unreachable itch inside her. To prevent myself from detonating inside her, I conjure up Erik's shit-eating grin as he admires his own reflection in the monitor during the few seconds of dead space preceding each showing of his new Olaffson commercial.

My present agency wasn't capable of producing anything good enough to wipe away that grin, but most New York production companies would at least listen to a spec idea from an on-staff creative like me working on an account like Olaffson. They were always keen to develop relationships that might lead to a lucrative job.

Above me, naked and shining, Yvette looked like she was peering into a well.

There was only one thing I was sure of.

I must not come.

I must not come.

I must not come.

I'd distract myself by thinking up commercials.

Open on a shot of a young man who looks exactly like Erik. He's playing the part of an Olaffson dealer as he hands the keys to a happy looking customer who looks exactly like me. We get a nice sleek shot of the car as I drive away.

The voice-over says: "At Olaffson our work doesn't stop when you buy a car." The car swings out of the dealership into the street and the Erik-alike follows alongside still waving. Cut to inside the car. "Yes, thank you . . . yes, thanks . . . good-bye," I say, but Erik is still hobbling along beside the car even though it's now starting to speed up. The voice-over continues: "Our after-care program ensures that you have a personal relationship with one of our staff who will help you with any questions that might arise."

In my role as the driver I wave good-bye to Erik in his role as the dealer and push the gearshift into drive. Close-up of my foot stepping on the gas; cut to a close-up of the speedometer pointing to 25 mph, but Erik is still out there. He's under pressure, but he's still there. Close-up of Erik's tie caught in the door.

The car brakes suddenly.
Our After-Care Service Goes Further: Olaffson.

Shuddering over me, Yvette leaned forward and exhaled roughly in my ear.

"Ohhhhhh, *oui . . . ouiiiiii.*"

I would have been very happy to go back to sleep, but I was now owed an orgasm. Declining her offer would be regarded as a callous misstep and would require a more carefully worded explanation than I was capable of delivering at that time in the morning.

It would be wiser to accept her manual advances. She had become very skilled in this department, so I knew it wouldn't take long and I'd make sure my gratitude was audible.

• • • •

The next day I was due to become a certified New Yorker. Not because my green card was about to come through—God forbid that should ever materialize—but because on Yvette's insistence, I would start seeing a therapist. She had decided that because I didn't share her enthusiasm for marriage, I needed my head examined.

Dr. Jessica Feldman.

I told myself that I'd be more open with a woman, but the real reason I chose her was because I could fantasize about fucking her. I already had a story in mind that would, I felt, set the tone for our sessions. It was a story that touched on many of the areas I felt were pertinent to my case and it would give her succinct overview of where I was coming from. A girlfriend invites her man to share his deepest, darkest fantasies. He is reluctant at first, since deep, dark fantasies are often best kept that way, but his girlfriend, intent on getting to know him better, assures him that no matter what he says, she won't be shocked, because after all it's just a fantasy. Falteringly he begins tell her about how he'd like to be gang-raped. By Japanese schoolgirls. Wearing strap-ons.

The girlfriend nods understandingly.

"Now you. What's your fantasy?"

It's her turn to be reluctant. "It's too . . . out there."

"Come on, I told you mine."

"Okay. To get married and have kids."

Yvette was simply not willing to continue seeing me until I dealt with my intimacy issues. Fearing an impending sexual embargo, I agreed. I wouldn't have even entertained such pusswhippery if she wasn't so sexually adept and in certain lights and on certain days and in her own way, quite beautiful in an unconventional sort of way.

When she turned up looking terrible, I'd feel a jolt of shame as if somehow it was my fault and carefully disguise the emerging grimace under a smile. And on the rare occasion she arrived looking carefree and beautiful, like a happy pretty sixteen-year-old, I'd stifle my glee. The idea being that either way I was expressionless.

Yes, I was looking forward to therapy.

Dr. Jessica looked directly at my crotch and played with her hair as I talked.

She was tall and thin and big-titted and always wore sensible gray skirts and jackets with shiny brooches and sometimes blindingly white blouses over those lovely bulging—oh, to do her. The knowledge that everything would need to take place within the allotted hour only heightened my fervor and fueled the fantasy even further.

"So, how was your week?" she'd say.

"Fuck my week," I'd say.

"Fuck *me* weak," she'd say.

I'd fold her over that big beige armchair and talk about my fantasies of fucking her *while* I fucked her. That would be worth the $250 a session at 8:00 PM every Wednesday and she wouldn't have to worry about cancellations.

But as she creased her smooth buttery forehead in my honor, I could sense her willingness not just to witness my pain but also to inhabit it. Between the filthy fantasies of what I'd do to her in our sessions, she somehow managed to point out patterns I hadn't realized were there. For instance, it was natural, she said, to emotionally and mentally shut people out, given that I had used a safety pin to physically prevent Brother Ollie from fondling my pre-adolescent balls. In other words, she said it was pretty normal to seek out similar solutions with anyone else who tried to *get in.*

Maybe my desire to butt-fuck, cock-spank, and ass-tongue her was an example of this. Thinking of her in such a light would keep even my therapist at bay. Why was I so distant? I felt like there might be an answer here.

She asked me to bring in the recently written ending to what I kept referring to as *my book*. I couldn't see how any of it related to our therapy sessions, but because I hadn't shown it to anyone else, I thought I might as well get some feedback since she was already on my payroll. And so in our next session after reading the last thirty pages of what would eventually become the ending of *Diary of an Oxygen Thief*, my therapist confidently proclaimed I was suffering from post-traumatic stress disorder. Whether it was caused by my childhood or my previous romance wasn't clear. Maybe both. At least she didn't say it was badly written.

• • • •

Yvette opened the door to her apartment before I got the key in the lock.

"I look like shit," she said.

The idea being that because she knew she looked like shit and acknowledged she looked like shit, she was relieved of any responsibility for actually looking like shit. If anything, it became my problem, since I was now expected to make her feel better about it. Whenever she kissed me, her hand would automatically stray to my dick

14

to monitor my affection for her. She hated when I got hard without her knowledge. But that night nothing was stirring, maybe because I'd spent the previous hour being investigated, or perhaps it was because she did indeed look like shit.

"You're not affectionate."

She had mentioned in an email that her stomach was acting up, so I summoned its power to my side.

"It's because your stomach is hurting. I didn't want to—"

"You're distant."

It was a question of theft. There was no hard-on where a hard-on should be. Ordinarily it wouldn't have been a problem. If anything, I was as surprised as she was. The long evening that followed was spent in silence, punctuated by the sighs of a martyr and the whipping back and forth of glossy magazine pages until at last she slipped wordlessly away to bed. I grabbed a pillow and a blanket and made for the couch.

The next morning I was woken by the sound of the shower being turned on and then off until finally she appeared in the living room in her uptight formal law-firm attire looking pinch-faced, unfucked, and even uglier than the night before.

Pausing at the door, she turned to look at me on the couch. "You can go back to bed now."

I was lying on a smoldering hard-on.

Pedophilic clergy, punishment beatings, mental abuse, domestic violence, two near drownings, and a recurring nightmare of the little boy I saw mangled in a farm accident.

"You had a brutal childhood."

Dr. Jessica looked directly into my eyes to make sure I heard her. There, it was official.

But none of it felt like it had happened to me. I was detached from these events. Had she confused my case with someone else's? Maybe she was exaggerating my trauma so I'd keep coming every week. And yet I began to enjoy our sessions mostly because it was becoming clear that I wouldn't be expected to marry Yvette. That I wasn't so much in love with her as too lazy to resist. But I wasn't about to marry her out of politeness. Why do that to myself? Or to her? She had her own agenda and her own time frame. She was thirty-three, so her body clock was sounding the alarm. I told Dr. Jessica about an unusually calm stretch of water on the Niagara River called the Deadline. Once you've passed it, there is no way to avoid the pull of the falls three miles ahead. I think we both knew I had said something significant, but that I was the one who needed to take action. Inaction would result in a marriage I didn't want to a girl I didn't love. A life I didn't want was already materializing around me. If I sat still, it would envelop me like a gas. And staying with Yvette after realizing this would be lying with my presence. I felt as though I had said all of this out loud, but I hadn't. Without looking up from her lap Dr. Jessica asked a seemingly unrelated question.

"Have you ever tried online dating?"

•   •   •   •

Yvette's recently becalmed hell-raising father was separated but not yet divorced from her bohemian-sculptor mother, who for some reason liked to argue in airports. Her ridiculously handsome father was a geologist and so, it could be said, was her privately educated sister, being as she was a professional gold digger. The grandfather on her mother's side made a fortune producing perfume and lived on what was essentially a private island north west of Bordeaux. The other grandfather was a retired judge in the French judiciary. He owned a summer house in the French Alps, where they holidayed at the slightest provocation. Yvette had been abandoned in her fair share of airports, and when she wasn't waiting in the lost and found, she was watching Papa chase Maman around their antique-laden home in Bordeaux with an ornate poker.

Her therapist forbade her from telling me too much about her upbringing, presumably because she thought I'd be shocked, but she couldn't have known that having experienced certain childhood eccentricities of my own, such nursery tales had a certain soothing effect on me. Anyway, by the time I was formally introduced to Maman I was adequately prepared to face the mass of neuroses, complexes, impulses, and moods that now stood collectively before me.

"Bonjour, I'm Veronique. It's so nice to meet you."

With her lantern jaw, close-cropped fair hair, and weathered skin, she looked more like a Scandinavian farmer than the mother of a junior lawyer for Leclercq & Menard.

I had already heard about the legendary debates with airport staff, the aborted attempts to liberate cute little penguins from zoo enclosures, and the commandeering of microphones from singers considered unworthy of the title. She bent almost in half to kiss me.

Veronique was a sculptor. A pretty good one, actually. Her pieces, to my eye, seemed heavily influenced by Picasso, but I didn't dare tell her that. I didn't want my first words to her to be confused with an accusation of plagiarism. We were en route *en famille* to the Metropolitan Museum of Art to see an exhibition of paintings by Gauguin, because logically enough, he was one of Veronique's favorite painters.

Yvette, though nervous about this meeting, was pleased it was happening. She had wanted us to meet at Thanksgiving, but this idea had proved too much for me, loaded as it was with so much significance. I knew that meeting parents, or even one of them, at Thanksgiving was tantamount to a marriage proposal. Even if the celebrants were French and Irish, there was still an unspoken implication that I was agreeing to something other than just a plate of turkey. But a visit to the Met was okay because it had plenty of emergency exits.

And Gauguin was a hero of mine too, since he'd given up his job as a bank clerk to shag French Polynesian girls. Confronted suddenly by a life-size sepia photo of the artist's tight-faced wife and children, I felt like I had just arrived home late with two strange Frenchwomen, and what time did I call this and was I not ashamed of myself? "Can't blame him for leaving," I said, and immediately regretted it.

It was exactly the wrong thing to say, touching as it did on Yvette's sensitivity about being abandoned. I braced myself for the public humiliation that would surely follow.

Surely Veronique would put me in my place. I myself was about to become an exhibit.

"Ahh, she is so afraid of being abandoned, no?" said Veronique, bending even deeper now to kiss her daughter. Yvette's cheeks beamed embarrassment outward into the exhibition space, and I suddenly realized Maman was Papa too.

She had to be, because Papa had fucked off. I'd heard all about his affairs with girls half his age and how Yvette was forced to compete with them for his affection. Papa was talked about with regret. But Gauguin had fucked off and they called him a genius. He can't have been the most

19

considerate of men to dump his wife and kids and take off with Van Gogh, that other famous family man. Gauguin's abandoned wife took the children to live with her wealthy parents, so therefore they were well cared for. And to be fair, they looked pretty fucking boring compared to the Technicolor windows into paradise on the walls ahead.

I refused to believe that he wasn't fucking every little Polynesian trollop he could get his hands on. Painting all day between orgasms and shagging all night between paintings. Should we think less of him because he didn't have a family? An emotional life? Or was he able to achieve what he did because he was free of such constraints? Art historians count him among the most notable post-impressionists, but to me, his most significant achievement was that he lived in an aftershave commercial before aftershave existed.

"You have found she can be difficult, no?"

We were on the roof patio of the Met, and Veronique was talking about her daughter as if she wasn't standing next to her. I mimicked a man testing the ground with his foot and then leaned back in mock horror as an imaginary explosion leaped from the tiled surface of the roof garden. Veronique's smiling eyes met mine and we turned to enjoy Yvette's confusion. The moment felt good and strangely just.

This was my cue to produce the glossy book of Gauguin prints from my shoulder bag and hand it to Veronique. And let's be clear here. She was the mother of the best sex I'd ever had. Approval from mother meant more sex from the daughter. I was willing for the gift to be misconstrued as willingness to commit as long as it remained unspoken.

"*Pour toi Maman.*"

I had been forewarned that she loathed people who tried to speak French, but I had spent $175 on the book and I wanted my money's worth. Inhaling loudly and ooh-la-la-la'ing, she bowed to kiss both my cheeks again. Real full-on wet kisses, not makeup-saving facsimiles. She wiped my face like I was a rascal and stepped back to regard me.

Later, back in her apartment, Yvette put away her phone after a long muffled conversation in high-speed French.

The verdict was in.

"Maman says she thought you loved me passionately and that it was clear to her we would be married. She also said that she herself liked you very much and that you were obviously of superior intelligence."

The deafening roar of the waterfall grew louder.

I was numb as she went on to say that her mother's boyfriend was using the fact that she was too old to have children as an excuse to end their relationship. He was thirty-nine (same age as me) and she was forty-nine. Mother and daughter now shared the same fear of abandonment. Yvette was worried that Maman was on the prowl . . . with me in mind. It was true she flirted with me, but I just assumed that this was what French mothers did.

The sexual possibilities of being the filling in a mother-and-daughter sandwich were not lost on me, but such a scenario refused to ignite if you were flanked by your mother-in-law and wife.

• • • •

"Dare to be average," said Dr. Jessica.

Dare to give me a fucking break.

If I succeeded in being any more average, the likelihood of her getting $250 an hour would be somewhat diminished. We had agreed that I would write down my dreams, so when she asked me if I had anything for her, I took out my notebook and read her the following scenario.

"I'm setting out chairs in the gym for my Sunday-night AA meeting when I become suddenly conscious of making too much noise. I look around, and there between the stacks of chairs are at least seven or eight young boys arranged in sleeping bags on the floor. It's a strange sight, but I assume for some reason that they are a junior basketball team who made bad travel arrangements and need somewhere to sleep. As I continue putting out the chairs, they begin to wake up, and without speaking, they stand up and bunch together by the wall, waiting for me to finish. This is when I notice they have no arms. I wonder how their vests can possibly remain in place on those smooth rounded shoulders. And because they are well behaved and respectful, it somehow feels okay to introduce them to some of the AA members who by this time are starting to arrive. I feel proud of these boys even though I have no idea who they are."

"That's so beautiful," said Dr. Jessica. "Can you see what it is?

I stared at her.

"It's your subconscious telling you it's okay now to bring your younger self into the AA meetings. They have no arms because that's how you felt when that guy was touching you."

The boy was contacting the man.

I was astonished the she could get all this from a dream. It was true I had compartmentalized the whole Brother Ollie thing. Quarantined it. But maybe now it had lost its potential to contaminate.

Later that night, Yvette called me an asshole with such conviction I almost felt grateful to hear such an honest utterance. Advertising had all but gutted me of any genuine emotion. We had been talking about *us*. Or rather, *she* had been talking about us while I stewed.

"Do you want to be that guy who has to keep changing his girlfriend every three years?"

Silence.

"Because they'll all want the same thing."

Silence.

Every three years didn't sound so bad to me. If anything, it was a little optimistic.

I prayed that I might be struck in love with her. It would make life so much easier. She was a ready-made life in waiting. French, highly cultured, great in bed (if not a little demanding), with an aristocratic artist mother so well connected in France I could already see the scenic summers in the Alps, the publishing deals in Paris, and the French-speaking children showing me the contents of their mouths. But as I tried to talk myself into it, I just couldn't conjure the required flutter in my chest. Or if I did, it was more like a twitch. Yes, the sex was the best I'd ever had. No doubt about it. Guiltless soaring orgasms that felt like time travel. So what was wrong? Other girls I'd met were boring in comparison or older or uglier or worse—American. Was I was in denial? Would I only find out how deeply embedded I was when I tried to pull out?

I thought more clearly when we hadn't had sex.

In the time we'd been together, the orgasms were so intense and so regular they'd had the same effect as medication. Once every two days after meals; and depending on the dosage level, I'd see Yvette as gentle, beautiful, and kind and myself as loving, caring, and truthful. But now that she was on sexual strike, I couldn't find this girl or that guy. Maybe lust was all I'd ever felt for her. Had I mistaken the softening effects of postcoital afterglow for romantic love? I knew that there would be no sex if I couldn't at least pretend there was some emotion attached to it. Had I begun to believe my own lies just so I could continue to get sex? But now I had to smoke myself out. There was no point in making us both miserable just because she wanted to have a child. I knew I'd find it impossible to love a creature whose first act on entering the world would be to demolish the one thing I really did have genuine feelings for. Yvette's ass.

Open on a classroom full of boys supervised by a Christian Brother. He walks between the desks craning his head to read the copybooks and pauses to point things out. He stops next to a ginger-haired boy and slides in beside him. The other boys exchange amused looks. Beneath the desk in a close-up shot we see the priest's hand emerge from a pocket slit in the side of his gown and crab-creep toward the boy's crotch. The forefinger and thumb pull at the fly fastener, but it doesn't budge. He tries again. Nothing. After one more tug we notice the boy's zipper is pierced by a safety pin. Cut to a close-up of the boy's face as he allows himself a barely perceptible smile.

Forty-Pack of Safety Pins, Extra-strong.

Browsing menus of single willing women was intoxicating at first. Pornographic, even. Beautiful girls with cocked heads and laughing eyes competing for my attention in a modern-day harem. I toiled over half-written messages and deleted them in disgust only to start anew. Finally after agonizing over every comma, period, and apostrophe I'd send out a message like a dove into the night. Annette87 was absolutely gorgeous, but believe it or not, it was not her beauty that caught my attention. She listed Francis Bacon, a contemporary of Shakespeare, in her *last great book I read* section and for *the superpower you would most like to possess,* she'd answered, "I'd like to read minds." So yes, I wrote her a poem.

Look ye to these blackened leaves,
Deathly froze 'neath icy screen,
Neglected thus by suns and moons,
These worried words seek news of you,
Thine eyes to them are planets bright,
Whose orbit brings the gift of life,
Sayest not thou art bereft of powers sublime,
Thou canst read words and therefore minds.

No reply. Maybe she never received it. Should I send it again? Maybe the Internet was down. In many ways a fleeting glimpse of a beautiful girl in the street was more merciful. You saw her and she was gone. Here you could ogle what you couldn't have for days on end. Meanwhile, capitalizing on your disappointment, ads for cars, aftershave, and clothes promised to make you more attractive. But I wasn't about to give up.

Intelligence, wealth, wit, and height.

These were the most commonly sought qualities on datemedotcom. I already had three of them, and I could mimic the fourth in the right shoes. I was never going to attract many replies on my looks alone, but I was confident that most girls were going to at least feign interest in a guy who made $250,000 a year as an advertising art director.

And having worked with some of the best digital retouchers in the world I couldn't help but notice that many of the photos had been modified. Skin lightened (I kid you not), blemishes blended, legs lengthened, weight reduced, stretch marks removed.

After I had been on only a few dates, it quickly became clear that if a seemingly gorgeous twenty-five-year-old girl was willing to meet a guy nearing forty, it meant he was going to have to pull up an extra chair for her ass. Witnessing a girl rearrange the table in front of her as she waited for her anatomical entourage to catch up was not something I wanted to repeat. I felt like the victim of a crime but with no emergency number to call because legislation had yet to catch up with whatever this was.

Scrutinizing the profile photos even more carefully, I realized to my horror I had been deceived by three very basic methods of in-camera trompe l'oeil.

1. Lying facedown on a plush carpet absorbed all manner of immensity. 2. Holding the camera up high created a false perspective that funneled even the most amoebic madness into a neat vanishing point. 3. Posing between two friends converted a milk-churn silhouette into an hourglass figure. I was looking at this all wrong.

Instead of being the customer, I needed to become the product. Instead of buying, I would sell.

At first I didn't catch the significance of profile names like Erin76, Shannon12, and Colleen111, but it soon arrived in me like a smile. As a walking, talking, realistically rendered, three-dimensional, life-size export of that mythical faraway land called Ireland, I had something to sell after all. These misinformed females, having grown up with stories of the old country strained through generations of omission and embellishment, were ripe for the romantic advances of a native-born Mick.

An Irishman with a girl's name?

Yes, that's going to be my headline for this email. You probably get a lot of messages (gorgeous girl like you), and as you trawl through them going DELETE, DELETE, DELETE, I thought I'd at least grab your attention with an eye-catching line . . . and let's face it, it must have worked, because you're still reading. But why would my parents give me a girl's name? Well, since they had me late in life

they knew I'd grow up with less attention than my siblings,
and like Johnny Cash sang in "A Boy Named Sue," the
hope was that I'd grow up independent and tough (imagine
the playground taunts). Did it work? You can judge for
yourself when we meet.

Girlsname

At first I only copied and pasted this message to girls who referenced Ireland in their profiles, but pretty soon I began to send it out randomly. Why not? Irishness was attractive to all cultures except the British, and there weren't too many of them over here. And anyway I could always screen the responses later. The objective was to see just what kind of quality I could attract.

It was revealing how grateful they all were, beautiful or not, for being referred to as *gorgeous.* Seemingly, this was enough to blind them to the fact that what they had received was a form letter. And almost all of them wanted to meet or at least learn more about the man behind the message.

"You have two new messages. First message."

Beep.

"*I hate you . . . I hate you . . . I hate you . . . I hate you . . .*
I hate you . . . I hate you . . . I hate you . . . I hate you . . ." The recording went on like this, with a few breaks for inhalation, until the tape ran out.

"New message."

"*I hate you, I hate you, I hate you.*"

Yvette had obviously felt a need to underline the passion of the first message with the comparative composure of the second. Why was she so aroused? Talking on the phone earlier, I had made the mistake of mentioning Dr. Jessica's suggestion that I might want to think about online dating, and she immediately hung up. Which was just as well because I was about to remind her that it was she who insisted I see a therapist in the first place. Dr. Jessica hadn't insisted I try online dating but because the idea had come from her I could present it as my therapist's suggestion. She had handed me a golden safety pin. When Yvette called again I let the call go to voicemail. Twice. When I felt an urge to call her back I listened to those messages. They became my equivalent of a picture of a fat person on the fridge.

In our next session Dr. Jessica said I looked for conspiracy everywhere. "Whenever you're stressed or overworked, you look around for the enemy. That's your pattern. You learned it from childhood—abuse from your teacher, denial from your mother—and now you're doing the same thing with this guy Andy."

Andy was the creative director on Olaffson, who very rarely left the building. It seemed to me that if you were any good at what you did, you should be able to go home every now and then. But not Andy. On weekdays we worked into the early hours; on weekends we just worked late. He needed me there because of my experience writing TV commercials, and yes, I had a better showreel than he did, but was there really any need for us both to be there at one AM on a Saturday morning? Throughout the working week, presumably for the benefit of the junior creatives, he'd try to make it all seem as if we were two friends hanging out. Just two guys checking out chicks.

"Look at that ass," he'd say as one of the junior account girls walked by. "Look at the swagger, it's innate."

"It's a nine," I said.

He shook his head in awe. "That's why they pay you the big bucks, buddy."

I had actually misheard him and thought he'd said "an eight," but I wasn't going to tell him that.

I suddenly saw through him. Why go home to a complaining wife and screeching kids when you could hang out in a trendy office with gorgeous account girls and your witty Irish art director? I was his creative butler.

I assured Dr. Jessica that I'd welcome the idea of being fired, but she sighed loudly.

"I'm sorry. You're stuck."

This new candor amazed me. Was it some sort of technique used by therapists? Remain silent for the first five sessions, then open up with all sorts of observations?

And by encouraging me to remain employed, was she

31

thinking not just of my job but her own? I was, after all, her misery-mortgage.

"You look smaller this time. Last week you seemed taller, you stood more erect, you had greater presence."

This wasn't at all like her. Ordinarily she was much more tactful about making comments of any kind. I didn't have the heart to tell her that last time I'd worn my Brothel Creepers. They add at least an inch to my height. I was sparing my therapist's feelings now? This was the equivalent of neatening the apartment before the cleaning lady arrived. Something was wrong. When I first lowered myself into the chair at the beginning of that session, the cushion and armrests were scorching hot. Reevaluating my near collision with a huge mannish-looking woman in the hallway, I couldn't help but wonder if it was possible to inherit some of the mood from the previous session.

"Look," she said, shuffling forward in her seat, "what do you do when you come to a fork in the road?"

Was I expected to answer? "Take it."

I was paying $250 a session for this? Previously, she had appeared all the more intelligent because she had said so little.

BRIDGIT

Bridgit's invitation to inspect the Celtic pendant around her neck allowed me to touch her cleavage, which ignited the kiss that led to her bed, where in the throes of fucking her, I noticed a picture of her dad on the bedside table.

He looked exactly like me. My thin-lipped and blue-eyed head lurched forward to eclipse his before retreating into the dark and reappearing.

Still a novice, not just to online dating but dating in general, I agreed to meet her mother, who lived in Syracuse, mainly because she promised all manner of sexual activity on the train there. Feeling slightly cheated after a less-than-exhilarating train ride, during which she made me come under a newspaper right there in the seat as pylons and ticket conductors rushed past, I arrived at Bridgit's childhood home. As the front door swung open I pretended not to notice her mother's expression of euphoria, when wide-eyed and hungry for her returned husband, she welcomed me into her house.

Surely Bridgit had sent her my photo.

I sat at the head of the kitchen table with Nuala, the younger sister, on my left; Bridgit on my right. Mom sat at the other end, flanked on one side and then the other by Paddy the dog. On the wall, Dad looked down on us from a portrait within a gold frame. He also looked down from the fridge, from the hallway, and even from a picture in the toilet, where at one point I sought refuge. But there was no escaping it. I was Dad.

Bridgit became spokesperson.

"So what do you think of Nuala's progress? Is she heading in the right direction?"

Everyone at the table blushed and looked at Nuala.

Silence descended. Whether I liked it or not, a scenario had unfolded around me. It was improv theater and I was up.

"She still has a few years to fuck around," I said.

This was met with squeals of delight.

"And the dog?"

"He looks fine to me. A bit chubby maybe."

"And what about Mom?"

"I'd do her."

Hysterical laughter punctuated by handclaps.

Bridgit respectfully requested that I remove my profile from datemedotcom and I respectfully intimated that I might like to keep it up and that was pretty much that until we met again two years later.

• • • •

In what turned out to be my penultimate therapy session I found myself telling Dr. Jessica that everything had improved, that my fear of intimacy was obviously due to my paranoia and that my paranoia was a result of being abused and that yes, it was still there, but I was now able to recognize it for the burden it was, as opposed to the good counsel I had imagined it to be. I acknowledged that as a kid I had drawn a map that accurately reflected the world around me, and though it had been a very useful navigation tool at that time, thirty years later I was still using it and wondering why I was bumping into things that according to the map shouldn't be there.

I heard myself acknowledge the success of the sessions while indicating a desire to end them. I shared with Dr. Jessica my vision of a therapy-free existence where it was possible to be well adjusted without a weekly outpouring of neuroses and cash. I told her, perhaps too honestly, that I spent the intervening days thinking about what to say in the next session so that we wouldn't both have to endure the excruciating silences for sixty minutes. And then in an ill-fated attempt at alleviating the timbre of the room, I submitted a work-in-progress tag line that would work well on small-scale media like fridge magnets and bumper stickers.

I paused for effect.

"Therapy? Enough said."

She smiled at this. "You wouldn't stop going to AA, would you?"

Predictably enough, she began to suggest that I might want to continue the sessions precisely because they were working. I immediately felt uncomfortable. Guilty even.

Like I was suddenly extricating myself from a relationship, I waited for her to say I was using my safety pin technique on her. That I was being distant. That she hated me. I didn't want to continue seeing a therapist when I was already going to AA meetings. Anyway I felt that what I'd gotten from her was about all there was to get. I did have to admit, though not to her, that I could see the logic of continuing the sessions, since they would at least provide me with someone to bounce ideas off of. Someone who could prevent me from making a mistake. Like discontinuing therapy.

NORA

I agreed to meet Nora on the steps of a church on Eighteenth Street, not knowing she would lead me led me inside to attend a mass that was just starting. Imagining all manner of pagan possibilities, I was happy to oblige. But once we were inside the cavernous candlelit interior, it quickly became clear that six o'clock mass was a gay singles scene where well-dressed young men eyed each other up between the benediction and the consecration. My father would sooner die than live in a world where this could happen. In fact that's exactly what he did.

But Nora didn't seem to notice. She was there to imitate her version of an Irishwoman. To her it was just a look, like dressing up as a cowgirl or gypsy. An excuse to wear tweed. She was in a Catholic church among figures both kneeling and standing, and that was enough for her. It was Ireland by Tommy Hilfiger. Apparently she had gone on a few dates with some guy called Ray. It was pretty clear he hadn't fucked her yet, but she mentioned his name often enough that it was clear she wanted to see how I'd address my competitor. This was more of her Irish posturing. I needed to win her. If she hadn't been so pretty I wouldn't have bothered. I emailed her that night.

On the west coast of Ireland, in a city called Limerick, in the shadow of King John's Castle, a black leafless tree inclines itself toward the orange glow of a streetlamp. In the absence of any natural source of light, this gnarled trembling hand reaches for the nearest manufactured equivalent. To imagine so natural a yearning squandered on so cheap a facsimile is too heartbreaking to contemplate, so instead, dear Nora, let us turn our attention to the future. Yours and mine. But before we do that and to help you adjust, we might need to get you some Ray-Bans.

When I did eventually get her clothes off she was as pale as a corpse. And she pretty much behaved like one. She lay there looking up at the ceiling as if she hadn't noticed I was about to fuck her. I thought about coming on her face just to see her expression, but since she had obviously gone to all the trouble of waxing either side of her jet-black bush, I thought I might as well go down on her. Pretty soon she wouldn't shut up. "Thank God. Thanks be to Jesus. Oh, thank God!" It was as if she had misheard the instructions. *Oh Jesus* or *Oh my God* was fine, but *Thanks be to Jesus* was just frightening. I felt the sting of her juices on my just-shaved face.

"Oh, poor thing," she said after a while. "Don't worry, I never come, it's the antidepressants."

SHEELA

Viewed from the front, Sheela was very aristocratic looking, but as soon as she turned even slightly sideways, there was a dizzying moment of refocus while her nose announced its dimensions—not unlike an aerial view of a ship's mast. She had lovely clean pale skin (her parents were Irish) and a beautiful, compact little ass. Tragically though, her hips protruded like an anorexic's. Was I after a relationship or a few fucks? This was a constant source of concern for her. She was looking for chemistry, I was looking for biology. She smiled dreamily into baby carriages, I winced at the back of her head. It occurred to me that had her nose been any bigger and my dick any smaller, a blow job would have been impossible. In the end it was academic. I knew we were finished after a particularly frustrating session trying to keep up with her breathless directions on how to fuck her. She eventually came very loudly, but far from the audible reward I had hoped for, I was sure I heard her say, "Blaahhhhh . . . blah."

It summed up our time together.

FRANCESKA

I decided I would never see her again before she even sat down. Her profile picture showed a beautiful girl in a white

T-shirt and high heels taking her own photo in a full-length mirror. The scenario had a Helmut Newton–esque feel to it, and I assumed this was why she had used the old Leica to capture it. A witty prop for a tongue-in-cheek shoot. Because she had described herself as a hybrid photographer/assistant/ model/writer, it made sense to present herself in this way. It also made perfect sense to meet her at a fancy coffee shop that served overpriced lattes in chipped, barely washed mugs. But as she approached, I realized her decision to use the Leica was more than just a retro-chic affectation. It was a mask. A digital camera would have required her to hold it away from that face and allow us to see it.

She was a hybrid, all right. The world-weary face of an Irish politician surveyed the café from the body of a lingerie model.

"I'm so sorry," she said—I tried not to stare—"for being late. I couldn't find the place, I almost walked past."

"Don't worry, you're worth the wait."

A lie so enormous a car probably crashed somewhere.

"Thank you," she said, reaching into her shoulder bag. "*You* don't look anything like *your* picture."

I hid my rage as she took out a small black wallet and began to show me badly composed photographs printed on cheap paper. Even if she had been stunningly beautiful I would have been unhappy about this, but under the circumstances I was seething.

"Really?"

While she talked, mostly about her photography, I tried to summon a version of myself that could somehow ignore her from the neck up, or more precisely from the chin up, because there was something there casting a small shadow. I couldn't quite tell what it was, and though I wanted to study it, I didn't dare.

"Do you still want to meet in Ireland?"

She didn't actually have any Irish connections, but because she loved everything about the place we had already exchanged texts about a future romantic rendezvous in Deelford. I hadn't told her I was already due there the following week for a quick visit home before flying to Las Vegas for an Olaffson shoot. I had wanted to make it seem like I was planning a trip around her. But that was before we'd met face-to-face.

"Yes," I said involuntarily and threw in a nod to make it more believable.

"Yes? But it's very expensive? No?"

Was she was offering me an escape route or was she trying to get out of it herself? Or was she pretending she didn't fancy me so I wouldn't feel obligated? Or was she angling for a free flight? I couldn't read that face one way or another. The fact that she could use a camera to hide her face might well have been the reason she got into photography in the first place. There was an ad for cameras in there somewhere. You get more detail with a digital camera. I tried to summon a version of myself that could somehow see it as a large

40

pimple. A chin-nipple, perhaps, but it was useless. The wart wore the woman.

MOTHER

After an overnight flight to Dublin and a joyless train ride to Deelford, I was jolted from a virtual sleepwalk into the kitchen of my childhood home to find my brother and mother touching my jacket like Bangkok peasants. To save them the embarrassment of asking, I placed a fifty-euro note between the saltshaker and the sauce bottle and emptied my coat pocket of coins into my mother's wide expectant hands. This secured my first compliment.

"Doesn't he look great?"

This was the Ireland I remembered.

Before I'd even sat down, she warned me not to call the fire brigade, since the last time I was home, I had needed their services to extinguish a chimney fire. Having recently taken to counting each separate rock of coal, my mother was hardly going to welcome the cost of having the chimney swept. The last time I was home, already mindful of her sensibilities, I had placed one diamond-in-waiting on a single pathetic sputtering flame, but apparently the chimney couldn't deal with the increased traffic and the smoke began to back up. I had no idea the fire brigade charged by the hour. I thought they were a government service like the postman or the police. When I produced my laptop, it was met with oohs and aahs.

My mother began dropping the first of many hints that she needed to pay off a thousand euros on a car accident she'd caused. There was a silence after this, which I suppose I was expected to fill with money, and when I pretended not to understand, she stopped making me cups of tea. Brian said I was paranoid about my money, that I was obsessed with it.

"I'm not the one obsessed with it," I said.

There was another silence after that.

Due to the prohibitive cost of oil, the central heating was never on for more than an hour a day even in December. Brian had discovered that sleeping with a pair of underpants over his head afforded the warmth of a hat but with more ventilation. He helpfully began to explain that 70 percent of your body heat escapes through your head. He had obviously forgotten that it was I who told him this after wasting two years of my life in Minnesota. I was about to suggest he'd be even warmer if he shut his fucking mouth, but I didn't. I pitied him living in that house with that woman. Our mother.

She was really pissed off that her husband was dead. She couldn't see that she was in fact very lucky to have someone, anyone, at home with her, even if it was only Brian.

The house had gotten worse since Dad died. There were pockets of unwiped goo everywhere. It was all too familiar and yet it was like some sort of dream. Brian without a wife and my mother without her husband. They'd become a sort of sexless bickering couple and I was the umpire. In the mornings I'd hear them stiffly descending the creaking stairs. The undead.

I gave my mother an autographed copy of *The Potter and the Rose* and joked that it would be worth a fortune some day because it was a hardback and the author was quite reclusive. She was happy about this until she noticed my inscription wishing her a happy Christmas. I had obviously devalued it. I looked past her annoyance, as I had done so many times before, out the kitchen window at the black, defeated trees. For the first time in this house, I felt fortunate.

I could leave.

In the past she had bid me emotional good-byes every time I'd left home for art college in Limerick or London or, more recently, America. My tears became easier and easier to hide until there were none.

The constant state of sleeplessness caused by a combination of jet lag and damp drafts of unheated air was like a torture technique in which my eyes were sewn open and I was forced to watch something I didn't want to see.

My mother's decline and my brother's misery.

I got up early the next morning after another sleepless night and crept quietly around the kitchen so as not to wake them. The less conversation, the better. There were only two more days before I flew to Las Vegas, but I desperately tried to think of excuses to leave earlier.

I sat down heavily at the table, and I realized I was sitting in exactly the same spot when I first told my mother about Brother Ollie thirty years earlier.

I remember waiting as she drained yellowish-green water from a saucepan of boiled cabbage. I was about to inform on the coolest Brother at my school. At nine years of age I couldn't even be sure that what I was about to tell my mother was controversial.

Mostly I was looking for a reaction. Shock. Disbelief. Laughter. For all I knew I might have been leading him astray. After all, why would a man dedicated to God want to play with the thing I peed with? The only satisfactory explanation was that I was evil.

Some weeks after I had established the habit of going to school with my trusty safety pin in place, I experienced what I would later realize was a sexual stirring. As Brother Ollie approached, preceded by the smell of his hair cream and aftershave, I noticed I actually wanted him to sit beside me, to touch me down there. But he had given up on me. As he passed me by in favor of another in his harem I removed the safety pin. Just in case. This means that my very first sexual yearning was not only co-opted by the Catholic Church, it was rejected. I summoned my courage and told her. But the cabbage was more important.

"Oh," she said, "he's just being friendly."

She dissolved momentarily as the steam enveloped her. I was her fifth caesarean in a row. She barely had time

44

to heal between births. It must have been difficult for the surgeon to find fresh skin for his blade. Each of us literally left a huge scar on her. Mid-century Ireland was a moral Middle Ages where priests, nuns, brothers, and bishops were feared like the Gestapo and contraception was the stuff of science fiction. The way things were back then, she was lucky she didn't have four more children. So were they.

Open on a rainy farmyard somewhere in Ireland.

A potato grader juts half in, half out of a barn as underage workers try to keep pace with the conveyor belts. Cut to inside the barn, where a young boy forks potatoes into the funnel of a grader as other boys positioned on either side of the machine busy themselves separating rotten specimens from the healthy. They all wear hooded anoraks against the rain and black potato sacks around their waists like makeshift aprons. In a close-up we see the uncovered cog-and-chain mechanism that powers the conveyor belt. As the camera pulls back, we realize that the boy with the pitchfork leans dangerously close to it as he works. Another small figure scurries along in the rain, edging past the others as he makes his way toward the boy on the end. A shock of ginger hair protrudes from one of the hoods, and as we see his face, we realize it's the boy from the safety pin commercial. This boy has noticed something strange about the newcomer. His hood is larger and darker than the others, and oddly he carries a scaled-down scythe, which appears custom-made for his stature. Suddenly the conveyor belt lurches and shudders. Something is jammed in the mechanism. The ginger-haired boy looks in the direction of the upset just in time to see two little legs swing impossibly into the air and fall away again. The grader continues to lurch and grind until the ginger-haired boy finds the switch. There is no sign of the strange little hooded boy with the scythe. Voice-over: "Tragedy comes in all sizes, so keep protective guards on all moving parts."

Issued by the Irish Government for Safety in Agriculture.

My mother's technique for coping with the grief of losing her husband of forty-three years was to refuse food in the hope that she might join him. On her way up to bed on that last night before I left for Las Vegas, she carefully closed the living room door so as not to disturb my television viewing. As she grasped the knob and the door began to creak shut, I had the strangest sense that I was seeing her alive for the last time. In stark contrast to this, a memory of her whooping with laughter flashed into my mind.

What the fuck did I care about the television? I was only sitting there trying to postpone another sleepless night in my freezing damp bed. An urge to save her suddenly rose within me. I'd bring my intelligence, energy, and wit to bear on the situation.

I won't let you die, Ma. Don't worry, I'm here. I'll save you. But then I realized I was powerless. I couldn't make her want to live. It was her decision. The living room door was like a coffin lid closing over her.

• • • •

"You don't have a vocation, you should start a family."

Being sent home from a seminary before you'd taken your final vows was the kind of thing that was whispered about in fifties Ireland where having a priest in the family was better than a relative in government.

But for my dad it was not to be.

The bishop himself had just ordered my father to go forth and multiply. This was no mere whim; it was an ecclesiastical directive. If this had happened today, he probably would have signed up for online dating. The speed with which he found the one he wanted (and no, it wasn't my mother at first) seemed to suggest that he might have had his eye on her for some time. Brenda Sullivan was pretty and well off and promised to another. And it didn't help that her family was aiming higher than a failed priest. So when he received an invitation to her wedding, his faith quaked. Not good enough for the priesthood and certainly not good enough for the Sullivans.

"God only breaks your heart so he can get in," he would tell me many years later. The bishop was God's representative on earth and my father would do his bidding.

In broad-shouldered suits that hung vertically from his thin frame and well-spoken after his five-year stint in the seminary, he must surely have cut a dash in the countrified dance halls of downtown Deelford. My mother certainly thought so. She was taken with his manners and poise, and of course his looks. He and his two brothers had strong, intelligent, angular foreheads with brows that sheltered deep-set, mostly blue eyes, and whenever they met, they took turns throwing their heads back in loud, uncontrollable guffaws.

All dead now, of course. Except for Liam, the youngest brother at seventy-nine. My mother couldn't bear to let him into the house during those first few weeks following the funeral, looking as he did, so much like a skinnier, paler version of her dead husband.

He was like a ghost knocking at the door.

Her nickname for my brother was Flash, precisely because he wasn't. She complained constantly that he couldn't be arsed* to find real work and was therefore a depressing influence. And *divorce* seemed like such a glamorous term to use in connection with my brother because nothing had happened to him since—well, nothing had ever happened to Brian. Even his marriage seemed inconsequential. He was

---

* A common term used in Ireland to describe a lazy man is to say *He couldn't bother his arse.* But my mother's elegant reworking of the phrase reduced even the energy required to express the idea, not just communicating the concept but demonstrating it.

receiving back pay from fate. I once walked in on him in the toilet and found him pissing not into the toilet but in the sink. He did this so he could continue watching himself in the mirror.

It wasn't vanity so much as self-surveillance.

Directly after his divorce he was so bereft of ideas about what to do with his life, he was like a life-size doll between positions. Brian making a cup of tea. Brian watching TV. Brian sitting. Brian standing. Talk about teachable. If my mother hadn't managed to fuck him up the first time, she was getting a second shot at it. They very quickly became an eccentric modern couple. She brought over fifty years of marital experience to the table and Brian brought nothing at all. He didn't pay rent. Her friends remarked on how closely he resembled my father and how lucky my mother was to in effect have him back.

But she didn't see it.

When he drove me to the station on a morning so moist it might have been regurgitated, I was so elated at the prospect of leaving that damp, rotting ancient island I almost fell out of the car when it stopped. He mock saluted and drove away, eyeing himself in the re-angled mirrors.

But my little walk down memory lane wasn't over yet.

From the platform I could see the farm where Timmy was killed. Much was made of the fact that I broke into the farmhouse to call the ambulance.

Like it was an act of heroism. But I would have done

anything to get away from the image of my friend dangling by the throat with the hood of his duffel coat woven obscenely into his pale skin. Breaking a window was the cowardly thing to do. I should have stayed and helped him, since he was still breathing at that point. But as it turned out, there was no escaping the horror of that day. Turning around with the phone still in my hand I was met by an equally disturbing sight. One of the other boys, busy robbing the place.

As the train pushed the damp empty buildings aside I realized my Christmas had consisted of four freezing days and nights in a damp house with a bitter old woman and a divorced unemployed barman. No wonder I was relieved to get out. I left five hundred euros on the mantelpiece to ease my guilt. Brian joked that my sister and I should pay him, since he was basically running an old folks' home for one. He can't have known that if he had insisted I would have been happy to set up a standing order. I looked up and down the train to see if there were others like me who couldn't wait to leave this wet, washed-out, rained-on place. The train was full.

ERIN

Erin, a pale, raven-haired beauty who stared at me from the recently opened JPEG, was young. Twenty-nine is young when you're almost forty. I had already searched her email address in Facebook to see if I could pull up her profile. I wanted to see if she had a big ass in tow, and lo and behold, I found there was. The photo showed she was not as clear-skinned in the un-Photoshopped version of the photo she'd posted on datemedotcom, but her body was visible now, so this didn't seem to matter. I leered over her profile for a while before calling her. She had been married once before, she said, and now wanted kids. She had a little Chihuahua she'd bought from Puppies & Puppies. She was going to a wedding that Saturday and was doing her laundry on Sunday and hiring a car for the weekend. She lived in Hoboken, and though she loved having sex, she was allergic to condoms and so could do it only with a specific condom made from lambskin.

"They're expensive and not easy to get," she said.

"How much is expensive?"

"Twenty-five dollars."

"Each?"

"Yep."

There was something refreshing about her lack of finesse. She encouraged me to speak so she could hear my accent. She wanted me. Pure and simple. No games. She invited me to go to a wedding with her that Saturday. She certainly wasn't wasting any time. It would mean a two-and-a-half-hour drive with a six-month-old puppy on my lap and three hours being paraded around like a captured American serviceman. I was thankful to be able to truthfully tell her I was on my way to Las Vegas for work. This impressed her. She was not quite white trash but getting there. Off-white, maybe. Eggshell. She bemoaned the fact that she couldn't drink at the wedding since she was driving, but she would make up for it the following night. She'd recently had a few one-night stands with a Texan who bought drinks for everyone in the bar wherever he went. She said this kind of behavior embarrassed her, but she couldn't refuse a man who bought her drinks all night.

And yes, she had sex with him.

"Did you use a custom-made lambskin condom?"

"Well no, not that night, silly, we were, you know, drunk."

"I like the idea of the lambskin condom because as an Irishman it satisfies my desire to shag sheep and women at the same time."

"I'll pretend I didn't hear that."

"I'll pretend I didn't say it."

Hearing her laugh I imagined her covering our child's ears in her version of our future. Isn't Daddy awful? I had a headache after forty minutes of listening to her.

I had stayed that long only in the hope that I might step into the toilet for some phone sex. But she was obviously thinking further ahead than I was. She wanted to get into my genes. So when she asked if I had the Irish Curse, I pretended not to understand.

"Well, yes, I suppose I do. I'm an alcoholic. In fact I've

been in AA now for fifteen years." It seemed like as good a way as any to extricate myself.

"Good for you," she said, obviously winded. "Congratulations," and then after a pause: "Fifteen years? Why, how old are you?

"Forty-eight," I lied.

"Your picture looks a lot younger."

"Well, that's what happens when you don't drink."

Another pause.

"So you're fourteen years older than me?"

She was audibly disappointed. She had just lost a house in upstate New York, three children, two rabbits, and a dog. All I wanted was a wank, and that was still possible without her.

Open on a shot of a railway tunnel somewhere in Ireland.

Birds chirp, bees buzz as the voice-over begins: "At the age of sixteen you are legally entitled to two of life's greatest pleasures." Suddenly a high-speed train thrusts itself into the tunnel and continues to disappear into the small snug-fitting opening. The voice-over resumes with a snicker: "The other one is the Young Person's Railcard."

Cut to a still-life shot of the Young Person's Railcard with an ID photo of the same ginger-haired boy we saw in the farmyard commercial earlier. He has grown up a little and now sports ginger sideburns to match.

Irish Rail: How Far Will You Go?

I was so tired after my sleepless week in Ireland all I could remember about Aer Lingus Flight 1444 to Las Vegas was a very unattractive girl on my left saying there might be empty seats up front and a toddler imitating the sounds of someone being brutally killed on my right. From behind me, unseen knees pressed urgently into the small of my back. I must have passed out because at the moment of landing I jolted awake in a stupor of self-hatred and dissatisfaction in Las Vegas's McCarran International Airport.

A small, neat Mexican man in a suit waited with a sign on which the word *Miss* preceded my name. When I pointed at it, he just smiled like I was joking and continued scanning the incoming hordes for the real me. I stood there waiting for him to understand. He stepped away. I stepped closer. I was too exhausted to do anything else.

It took longer than usual, but when he realized his mistake he placed the sign in a nearby trash can and looked for a moment as if he might get in there with it. "I'm very sorry, sir."

Having established my identity he took me in his darkened car to a cultural abattoir known as the Merchant of Venice Hotel, where in room 1225 I made the mistake of thinking I could get through to room service. After enduring forty-five minutes of taped messages and bad ads I was so relieved to hear a live human being, I shouted at him.

When the halfhearted, half-heard apology ended, I was thrust back into Tele-purgatory, and I slammed the phone down in disgust. I picked it right back up again. This led to a conversation with my mother, who was at that moment watching reruns of *The A-Team,* and I knew without having to be told that I'd have to call her back. Far from wanting to hear her voice, I was determined to avenge myself on the agency by running up as big a phone bill as possible. I breathed and exhaled, breathed and exhaled, and tried again.

"It's freezing cats and dogs here," she said when I was at last deemed worthy of an audience. "What's it like over there?"

But before I could answer, she began telling me how Murdock in *The A-Team* reminded her of Brian, and the rest of the "conversation" was about how sad it was that he couldn't get another woman and what did I think about that. Did I think he'd be able to get a woman through that thing that I did on the computer, because after all, I seemed to be doing all right by it, and let's face it, I was no looker. But again, before I could get a word in, she was off again.

"Do you know Mrs. O'Shaughnessy?"

"No, Ma, I don't think so."

"You do, you met her."

"Did I?"

"Angela O'Shaughnessy."

"No, I don't know her."

"Married to Seamus O'Shaughnessy."

"I can't say I know her."

"You do, I'm telling you."

"Where does she live?"

"Donaldstown."

"I don't know where that is."

"You do, you do. We were there once."

"Does she have red hair?"

"No, you bleddy eejet, that's Geraldine. You said Angela had to throw her boobs over her shoulder before she could tee off."

"Ahh, yes. Now I have her. Yes, what about her?"

"She's dead."

Now I wanted to shout at her too. I actually did a couple of times, but my cell phone service provided gaps into which my expletives fell and rendered me civil. Not that she would have noticed—she just kept talking and talking as I paced around the horror that was my room: imitation books fashioned from fiberglass, mass-produced carpets with badly done fleurs-de-lis, and marbling even on the air conditioners.

I had to get out. But I soon learned my room was tasteful compared to the rest of the city. Standing outside the hotel in the blazing sunshine, I could see only too clearly now the full-scale fiberglass replica of St. Marks Tower, with its digital screen looming over plastic gondolas, operated by stocky blond women in khaki cutoffs. The canals looked like they were filled with blue paint, and for all I knew maybe they were.

On that short, unforgettable walk to a desperately needed AA meeting I encountered scaled-down versions of the Eiffel Tower, the Brooklyn Bridge, and yes, the Great Pyramids of Egypt. Why visit Paris, New York, or Cairo when you could pose in front of these effigies and save yourself the journey? A digital crawl attached to a skyscraper announced: "Paintings by Pablo Picasso . . . Édouard Manet . . . Paul Gauguin . . . and many . . . many . . . more."

My old friend Gauguin, here?

Seeing the names of these artists presented in the same manner as Tony Bennett got me thinking that it would be great to enclose Las Vegas in a glass dome and present the entire city as a postmodern post-ironic work of art. A geosphere of what not to do.

A metropolitan objet trouvé.

But this wasn't art. It was life. My life. And I hated being in it. I was being swallowed whole by a sort of daylight darkness. This wasn't just a job any more. It was a condition where affection, friendship, honesty, and kindness were co-opted to lever a purchase. I needed an AA meeting. On the way there I called my sponsor and begged him to let me quit my job.

"Go in until lunchtime tomorrow," he said, "and call me then."

Open on a shot of me hard at work in an office setting. The tinny sound of music from my headphones is interrupted when we suddenly hear a booming voice.

"Sell. Your. Apartment."

Maybe I downloaded something weird. It's probably some creative real estate commercial aimed at iPod users. I shuffle to the next track.

"Sell. Your. Apartment."

I remove the headphones. Strange. Maybe there's a virus in my computer. I carry on working until lunchtime, and just as I'm about to get into the elevator I hear the voice again.

"Sell. Your. Apartment."

I look at the guy in the elevator beside me. "Did you hear that?"

"Hear what?"

"A voice saying, 'Sell your apartment.'"

The guy looks disappointed in me. This continues over the next few days. I hear the voice saying the same thing at the most unexpected times: on the toilet, just before going to sleep. Cut to a SOLD *sign being taken down outside my apartment. The voice seems to have stopped until . . .*

"Empty. Your. Bank. Account."

By now I'm starting to look pale and exhausted.

In quick cuts I first enter and then exit a bank with a suitcase full of cash. There must be $300,000 in there. In the park I take out a $100 bill from the case to buy a sandwich. I'm looking up now, waiting, hoping the voice will say something, but nothing happens. Some dodgy-looking characters starts eyeing me up.

I'm getting nervous. Finally the voice says "Flight." I get up and run. I'm followed by three sketchy guys who can't quite keep up. Cut to an airport departure screen: Flight 1266TRV

In close-up we see I have a matching ticket. The flight departs for Las Vegas. I have become very philosophical at this point. I fall asleep clutching the flight case. After landing in Las Vegas, I step out of the terminal, slip into the back of a cab, and wait.

"Where do you . . . ?"

I put one finger to my lips.

"Wait."

The cabdriver looks at me in the rearview mirror.

"The. Merchant. Of. Venice. Hotel."

"The Merchant of Venice Hotel."

Arriving outside the hotel I am welcomed by porters and ushered inside. Still clutching the suitcase, I once again wait for instructions, but none come. I wander around the hotel lobby, moving between the roulette tables and the slot ma-

chines. One hugely overweight man in a T-shirt that says IN THE ZONE *has fallen asleep in front of a slot machine. I look around desperately. What am I doing here? Maybe I'm losing my mind? I start to cry.*

"Third. Table. On. The. Right."

Without hesitation now I push through the gamblers till I reach a roulette table surrounded by people already in the middle of a cycle. The ball clatters to a stop, and two people walk away dejected, leaving a gap in the crowd. I heave the flight case onto the table. This must be it. The moment that makes sense of it all. I open the case and tip the contents onto the baize. There is a loud groan of pleasure from the onlookers.

"Put. It. All. On. Twenty-four."

I make an ineffectual attempt at grouping the cash into one area as if to ensure it straddles the number twenty-four.

"Red," the voice says.

Accordingly I shove the mound of money a little to the right.

"No more bets."

The croupier is adamant. The wheel is spun. All eyes on the little metal ball as it revolves inside the roulette wheel for what seems like an eternity. There is at least four hundred thousand dollars in cash on that table. People saunter over from other tables, and a quiet descends as the croupier flashes a look at the security

camera overhead. In black-and-white extreme close-up
we see the little metal ball bounce, hop, skip, skidder, and
wink. At last the wheel slows down and the ball seems to
be trying out random compartments for comfort before
leaping out to try another. Finally as the spinning sub-
sides, the individual compartments move slowly enough
to be discernible. The ball sits in a black compartment
numbered twelve. A collective groan rises from the spec-
tators and they immediately disperse as if such misfortune
is contagious.

"Aww, shit," the voice says.

The croupier drags the stack of money away from me and
begins stuffing it into the slot in the table. A title appears on
the screen. For more reliable investment advice, call Belve-
dere Bank Services 0800 244 78648.

JESSICA

"Now push your hips up to me because I want to shove
my stiff cock inside you . . . but I'm going to make you wait,
you'll have to beg me . . . I want to hear you beg me."

I held the phone to my cock so she could hear it squelch
as I pummeled it. "Can you hear that?"

Silence. She wasn't sure if she should be doing this, and
yet she wanted me to continue. "Yes."

"That's what your cunt will sound like when I fuck it
with my stiff cock."

"Ohhhh."

It was interesting to note that the word *cock* on its own didn't seem to have any effect until it was accompanied by the word *stiff*, *hard*, or *rigid*. A cock was just a cock, but a stiff cock was a compliment. The power of the adjective.

"Ohhhh."

I'd experiment sometimes and leave a long silence, inviting the caller to guess what I'd say next (I'd have to resist throwing in something surreal like *lawn mower* or *Tupperware* just to see what would happen). These silences would sometimes bring forth surprises.

"*I want you to come in my mouth.*"

The dirty little cunt. She would never have said that if we had just met in Starbucks.

"You're a dirty little cunt," I said.

"Ohhhh."

Over the public speaker system the stewardess asked passengers to return to their seats.

"You're on a plane? I've never done it on a plane."

"You have now."

As I left the toilet cubicle, I must have looked like I had just received some excellent news. This was better than real sex. I would definitely be calling her again. A JPEG arrived in my phone of a picture she'd taken seconds earlier, a close-up of two glistening fingers inside herself. We were approaching New York and I had a date.

DIANE

She turned up at Cafe Mozz looking so gorgeous and tiny and cute I absolutely wanted to have sex with her there and then in the street against a lamppost. In her profile, she looked like a ten-year-old boy with tits, so I was already a little ashamed of the explicit nature of my intentions toward her before she even turned up. But she seemed to enjoy the attention. Or was it my discomfort? She looked so young, a siren went off somewhere inside me.

She told me all her clothes came from the children's section of Old Navy, so she had become quite adept at removing decorative cartoon characters and bunny rabbits, but sometimes she said she liked to leave them on. There was a pause here as she waited for my reaction. *Sometimes she left them on?* Why would she tell me that? An unspeakable sexual sea creature caught the light for a second before slithering silently back into the murk. Such a sighting could never be reported. Maybe it was a diversionary tactic designed to distract me from the fact that her interest in me was purely professional. She couldn't mention that what she really wanted was a photo assignment, and I couldn't give voice to my illegal longings.

"I love your emails" was the first thing she said to me in person. This of course was clever of her, not just because it was flattering but because my emails to her had been predominantly erotic in nature.

Here are my balls,
This is my penis,
My hopes are high,
It'll come between us.

She let me believe I might have my way with her that very night if it weren't for the fact that she needed time to get over her ex-boyfriend. What she didn't mention and what I found out later was that she was already living with a man and would go home to him that very evening. She was very pretty in a pointy sort of way, and even though she did her best to behave like a lost little girl in a world of wonder, the prominent nipples under the tight white cotton of her skintight T-shirt seemed to suggest otherwise. That she had chosen among all the clothes in her wardrobe to wear such a revealing T-shirt to our first date gave me a thrill that must have informed my features. I assumed it was one of the items of clothing she had referred to earlier. And since I was the one doing most of the talking, the conversation seemed to sparkle. At the end of an excellent evening after a faux argument about who should pay the bill (I won), she jokingly punched the air between us and I angled my cheek mimicking impact. But misreading my intention, she leaned forward to kiss me there instead. Suddenly in danger of rejecting a kiss I hadn't expected, I clumsily kissed her cheek as she tried to kiss mine. This was particularly dishonest of her, since she had effortlessly conjured up one of those awkward romantic moments that so often occur between people still unsure of the others' affections. It seemed like a good time to tell her that I had been working too hard and it would be nice to slow down a little.

"Yes, you should be kinder to yourself," she said, ingratiating herself with someone who could lead to a seventy-thousand-dollar-a-day photo assignment.

"My first act of self-kindness will be to see you again on Wednesday night," I said, camouflaging my desire to rip off her child-size knickers and fuck what I found there.

"I'd like that," she said, blushing at her own dishonesty.

"Excellent," I said, mortified by mine.

I googled her name and a blog came up featuring the weekend trials of a fixer-upper as she renovated a place in Sag Harbor. There was a picture of her in a checked shirt cuddling a huge wild-haired fucker in a newly delivered claw-foot bathtub.

"Me and my man," the caption read.

The plumbing alone would cost a fortune.

• • • •

The following day, back in the agency, I was in the middle of printing out fifty pages of *Diary of an Oxygen Thief*, as requested by a potential literary agent, when suddenly standing there right beside me was Andy. He was waiting for something of his own to print and he just kept reaching for my emerging pages, scanning them and smirking to himself. I couldn't stop him. He was entitled to look for his printout. I couldn't stop the printer either. I would have pulled out the plug if I had known where it was.

Click, whir, *pffht*.

"*I liked hurting girls.*"

Click, whir, *pffht*.

"*Your cunt is loose.*"

Click, whir, *pffht*.

"*Call that a head-butt?*"

Slivers of my life being served up like prosciutto.

Eleven pages in the tray meant there were thirty-nine more to go. Sweet Jesus, make it stop.

"So. This is your big breakout novel?" He didn't look up from the pages as he spoke. I shouldn't have been printing anything that wasn't work-related. And yes, I could have waited till he'd left for the day, but he was always fucking there. Even on the weekends. Before I could answer, our account director Josh walked over with some other guy in a suit I'd never seen before. Andy looked quite handsome when he was enjoying himself.

"Do you want me to call you when it's done?" I hoped—no, prayed—that he'd have a modicum of respect and walk away.

66

"No, that's okay, I'll wait. So do you have a publisher?"

"Not yet, I'm sending this to an agent."

He raised his chin and smiled as if I had just explained absolutely everything that had preceded this moment in the history of time. I decided to walk away from the printer and hide in the men's room for a few minutes. When I felt enough time had passed, I'd come out and retrieve my vile manuscript and retreat to my office and call my sponsor and beg him to let me resign.

But after only a few seconds pretending to piss, Andy seemed to spring from the floor at the urinal beside me.

"So, do you have these in Europe?"

He was referring to the flushers on the urinals, which might or might not have been particular to the United States, and I suspected he already knew the answer before he asked me. I turned to look at him, mostly in disbelief. Was he going to work in some witty remark about me being flushed down the toilet and never getting another job again? This fucking guy.

I pretended to misunderstand. "Penises? Yes, we have them, but they're much bigger."

The easy smile froze. "Remind me not to set you up like that again," he said.

Had I lost my mind? This guy had the power to fire me. Without a job, I'd be an illegal immigrant.

Open on a shot of me with my own shoeshine stall. A suited executive is talking on his cell phone as I finish giving him a shine. The camera finds my forlorn face in the reflection of his shoe. In that same reflection somebody steps into view behind me. I look down at the pavement, and instead of another pair of men's shoes I see what appears to be a pair of ladies' high-heeled boots. But as the camera follows my gaze upward, we realize the girl is wearing a one-piece leather catsuit stretched tantalizingly over every contour of her gorgeous body. And though she's flawless in every way, the leather looks lackluster and uncared for. She needs a damn good buffing.

Keeping her eye on me, she gingerly steps up onto the shoeshine stand and dramatically dusts off the seat before lowering herself into position. Passersby stop to look at her. She's that beautiful. I try to remind myself that she's a customer, but it's impossible to hide the effect she's having on me. Is she naked beneath that body-hugging leather? Obviously enjoying my discomfort, she uncrosses her legs and offers me a foot. I reach for a piece of cloth, but when I try to spit on it I realize my mouth has gone dry. Unperturbed, she leans provocatively forward and offers me her bottle of Perrier.

Perrier. Thirst for Life.

MISS CANADA

But Andy didn't fire me. Instead I was assigned to oversee yet another shit commercial, this time being shot in Canada, where all five cars in the Olaffson stable demonstrate their snow-traction capabilities as they converge at a ski lodge for the holidays. Each member of this unlikely family drove an Olaffson, and it is only due to this fact that they could be together for the holidays. A lesser car would have careered off the road. This, it turned out, was the script Andy had been waiting for that day at the printer. And this assignment, it turned out, was his way of punishing me for being so brazen as to announce my ambitions of being a writer. All advertising creatives have at least one screenplay, novel, musical, play, or children's book hidden under the bed, but it's considered very bad taste to talk about it. Why talk of escape when you're in a maximum security prison?

The freelance producer found some idiot French-Canadian director to shoot it on the cheap because he was as desperate to get into the business as I was to get out of it. Before we even landed in Calgary I couldn't wait to leave. The director, Jean-Philippe, asked in his thick French accent if I needed anything shot for my reel. He must have guessed I was so bored with this shoot that he needed to offer up something extra to keep my interest.

Creatives often asked directors to shoot a personal project on the back of a fully paid-up production like this, but even if I had something I wanted shot, I wouldn't have trusted him with it. But because he was eager to please us anyway, he had already thought of something else. That same evening after the so-called shoot (it was all over after two hours), our client Ken (or No-Ken-Do, as I called him), our freelance producer (I forget his name), and I were picked up in a huge SUV outside the hotel and taken to Calgary Adult Club, courtesy of the desperately bored director.

Within seconds of being ushered into the VIP area and offered drinks I didn't want, I realized I had no prior reference for a rabbit-fur bikini. Why would I? It had never occurred to me that a bikini could be made from such material. It wasn't practical. It contradicted itself.

It was like a candle lit by a lamp.

The contrasting textures of fawn-colored fur and the clean, nearly translucent skin almost got me going. I say *almost* because the lighting was too harsh and the interior too cavernous, and let's not forget that getting even a hint of a hard-on in the same room as Kenneth Berg, Olaffson's recently promoted marketing director, was an imponderable.

"She's a former Miss Canada," he said while peering at me out of the corner of his eye. I could hardly believe it myself as I risked a sideways glance of my own at the phallic tower of red casino-style chips surging upward from his table, representing only too graphically his desire for the alarmingly young girl on the stage in front of us. As he lobbed, flicked, and tossed these wooden disks, the artist formerly known as Miss Canada positioned herself expertly to catch each filthy thought above her now fur-free and hairless vagina. This, it turned out, was Canada's real attraction. Not the strength of the dollar or the endlessly available snow, but the fact that the strippers were allowed to go nude.

"In Canada the beaver goes free," said No-Ken-Do, who at that moment was busy scrunching up his nose like he was making faces for a baby. But her vagina was dry and uninterested. I knew this because I could see right into it.

Its owner made absolutely no attempt to appear aroused by what she was doing, and as a result, neither did I. I slipped away and hailed a cab back to the hotel, where I had a Posh Wank (I used a condom) and fell asleep sideways, still clinging to my dick. In a dream I was reciting a customized version of the right-to-bear-arms motto—*You'll have to pry it from my cold dead hands*—when I was awoken at four AM by a knock on my door.

"Your early morning call, sir."

The producer must have arranged it, because apparently I was due to fly back that same day. And so it came to pass that a third of the way through a half-understood five AM flight to New York, I was stopped by immigration officers in the Toronto airport.

"I'm sorry, sir, your visa has expired."

I feigned wakefulness.

"My what is . . . what?"

The producer had already gone ahead and I couldn't call him because my phone was dead and now I was being escorted away and my bags were being recalled. I remember feeling only the beginning of a surge of panic, which then immediately subsided and settled back into what could only be described as relief.

Something significant was happening.

My work visa was out-of-date, and there was no way, especially in the post-9/11 environment, immigration was going to let me back to New York, where, set loose among the unsuspecting public, I might put the finishing touches to yet another crap commercial. They were right. I had to be stopped.

"So I can't go back to New York?"

"No, sir. You're staying in Toronto."

Harsh punishment indeed. I was shown into a window-less room where a huge testicle-faced man in a blinding white shirt did his best to behave like he was asking trick questions.

"But you just said you'd flown in from Calgary."

"Yes."

"So where were you going?"

"New York."

"What for?"

"I live there."

"But you have an Irish passport."

"Yes, but I live in New York."

"And you say you were shooting a commercial."

"In Calgary, yes."

"What do you do?"

"I'm an art director."

"What does that entail?"

"Making the copywriter look good."

His eyes remained on my passport.

"And you don't drink?

"What? No."

"Nothing at all?"

"No."

"Not even at Christmas?"

"No."

"And you're Irish?"

"I *am* Irish."

"*Conas a ta tu?*"

Were they fucking serious? I was being asked questions in Gaelic now?

And how did he know I didn't drink? Had they looked up my profile on datemedotcom? It is true that anyone growing up in Ireland would have at least a rudimentary understanding of Gaelic, but how the fuck did he know that?

I had always been terrible at Gaelic. I never managed to get even a pass on all the test papers I'd taken, and now because I couldn't think of the response to this basic question, I was going to be incarcerated in Canada.

Slowly from somewhere uninvited, maybe because my internal editors were not yet at their desks, a deep sense of dread began to overtake me like some huge abstract ink-stain widening within me.

Would I be strip-searched by this gargantuan?

Each of his fingers was bigger than my dick. He reached into a drawer where I suspected he kept his rubber gloves.

I was about to lose my virginity to a Mountie.

He took out a stapler.

When I was finally allowed to make a call, I was so happy to hear our receptionist mispronounce the initials of the agency (there were too many egos jostling for attention), I almost cried. She put me through to our legal guy, and suddenly it was as if the Lord God Himself spake unto me.

"We've had this happen before. You can help Silvestro and Lucien in our European office while we figure this out."

It certainly seemed like a reasonable solution, but I was surprised he was able to suggest it with such confidence. My Irish passport allowed me to work anywhere in Europe, but did the agency lawyer have the power to just send me there?

Surely such an idea would need to be run past Andy. Unless of course he already knew about it.

Either way, I had just agreed to be sent to the most precarious place on the planet for a recovering alcoholic and budding sex addict. Or the most convenient, depending on your point of view.

2

Hi, I'm a writer newly arrived from New York, and I'm sitting out here on the balcony of my Prinsengracht office looking out on the canal. As I type this, I'm having to half close my laptop because there's a squirrel (or at least I hope it's a squirrel) above me munching on something left out by my upstairs neighbor, and as a result there is some serious crumb-spillage onto my keyboard . . . so if I stat to moss up my werds as I tip I'm hape you'll firgove me??? But what has all this got to do with you?? Well, I don't want you to feel bad, but I'm supposed to be working on my second book, the Notoriously Difficult Second Book (hey, that might be a good title), but after seeing your beautiful picture, my concentration went out the window.

You could say I'm out here trying to find it. Write soon or
I won't be able to."

The profiles in the Amsterdam section of datemedotcom were mostly made up of Eastern European immigrants and British expats working for international companies lured there by tax concessions. And if one could judge from the repeated references to books, films, and music by artists like William Burroughs, Lars von Trier, and Leonard Cohen, it was obvious to even the untrained eye that a morbid intelligence prevailed. Unlike their American counterparts, who took great pains to appear companionable and contented, the attitude here was openly suicidal.

Maybe it was all that rain.

I had hoped that my impersonation of a happy-go-lucky newly arrived writer might go some way toward alleviating the mood, but my empty inbox seemed to indicate that I would have to do better than squirrels if I was going to get laid in Amsterdam. And yes, the red-light district was minutes away, but paying for sex was unacceptable. It took all the charm out of it. If anything, it was too honest.

Earlier that Sunday afternoon, before letting myself into our elegant Prinsengracht offices, I attended an English-speaking AA meeting on the Oudezijds Voorburgwal (good luck pronouncing that), and after a brief conversation with a local man called Cyril I was able to glean that online dating wasn't nearly as accepted in Amsterdam as I had hoped.

In fact when Cyril finally managed to absorb the idea into his comprehension, his nose twitched involuntarily like he had just smelled something awful in the air around us.

This reaction from an alcoholic/ex-junkie/wife-beater proved that online dating didn't just reek of desperation. It was worse than that. It smacked of America. Meanwhile these immigrant girls were unfucked and far from home in a country where it rained constantly and fits of coughing stood in for conversation. Of course they were miserable.

From downstairs, the sounds of pedestrians on the Prinsengracht mingled for a moment with the muttering of two men's voices before the front door closed again.

Next came an insistent pounding, which I quickly learned was the result of two people ascending the stairs. Lucien, with his black, lifeless eyes scanning the floor ahead of him, was first to enter the room, and he continued apparently unaware of my presence to his desk. Equally intense and similarly preoccupied, Silvestro Da Gemi, the black-bearded creative director of the Amsterdam office, followed in Lucien's wake.

I hoped that what I was witnessing was the silence that follows a heated argument, as any tension in their relationship might be an opportunity for me. But as I watched them settle into adjacent desks without so much as a nod of recognition in my direction, I realized I couldn't have been more wrong. In fact, the full measure of their collaboration would soon become apparent in the form of an award-winning ad campaign called *The Life Less Driven.* I coughed and shuffled in my seat, and when neither of them looked up, I had to assume I was being ignored and that my presence was indeed an inconvenience. It was true I had been sent there by their so-called superiors, but they were obviously above all that. This was Amsterdam. Lucien was a Parisian, Silvestro was a Roman, and I was just some guy who had fucked up his travel arrangements.

A homeless person.

Sat there bathed in the pink glow from datemedotcom's website, I understood now why Gertrud, our HR lady, had been so reluctant to give me the alarm code for the building the previous Friday. I thought it was because nobody worked weekends in laid-back Amsterdam; little did I know that it was because Silvestro and Lucien were coming in and obviously would not welcome distractions. I couldn't tell her I only wanted to check out the local pussy on my desktop, and she couldn't tell me they didn't want me working on the new campaign.

But I *was* there, and even though I wished I could disappear, I couldn't. I knew what they were working on because I had already been cc'd on the brief. It was the same brief as always: *Make Safety Interesting.* The office location might have changed, but Olaffson's creative brief remained constant. I was expected to work on it with them, but I knew they'd kill any idea of mine before I even uttered it. And yet if I was to justify being taken into their fold, I'd need to at least pretend to come up with something.

I stared at my screen.

Now I was miserable too.

Norwegian summers are short and the resident reindeer needs to make the most of the newly sprouted pastures. The more he fattens in preparation for the cold months ahead, the more attractive he becomes to the other local resident, the mosquito. Before long, the huge antlered animal is barely visible through a whining, hovering haze—not so much a reindeer being harassed by mosquitoes as a cloud of mosquitoes in the shape of a reindeer. The humidity combined with the moisture from the fjords provides the ideal breeding ground for the mosquito. And for the reindeer herders, a swarm of mosquitoes is better than a sheepdog. They wait, chatting and smoking on higher, cooler ground, for the exhausted beasts to shuffle meekly into harness. But this one, not content with being bullied uphill, kicks and bucks as he tries to unseat the multitude of insects. He escapes into sharp focus only to succumb once more to the blur. This is repeated until the energy expended requires a return to grazing, which is apparently unacceptable because suddenly the reindeer-shaped mosquito cloud ejects the real-life reindeer into one fresh, clean, breezy moment of freedom and into the fjord below.

YORTA

"I love the reindeer story I can definitely identify"

In all of Deadkween's very black-and-white profile pictures, she appeared luminously beautiful in sultry poses wearing an assortment of black leather and lingerie. In one particularly successful picture she paid homage to Charlotte Rampling's famous pose from *The Night Porter,* complete with long-sleeved evening gloves and Nazi hat. She was lost-looking in a soon-to-be-dead sort of way. As if her last earthy exhalation would be in orgasm. She owned a small gallery in Budapest called Poisoned Reservoir and visited Amsterdam regularly "for inspiration." She wrote poems and attached them to her handmade dead baby dolls. I was allowed to know this much over the phone, but she waited until we met to tell me she was an albino who dyed her hair black and wore contact lenses. I'd never met an actual albino before. She certainly was extremely pale, but no more so than I'd seen on a Dublin bus. It immediately explained why all her pictures were black and white and why she looked so good in them. At this point we were on her black leather couch in her black-walled apartment overlooking the Vondelpark, and though it was no more than 6:30 PM, it was almost totally dark in there because she'd draped veils over all the lights and closed the blinds. She could be exposed to daylight for only a limited length of time. All signs indicated that I was about to fuck my first vampire until I declined a beer in favor of a water.

"You're not in AA, are you?"

"Well, actually, yes, I am."

I left a gap for the inevitable gush of admiration.

"I. Fucking. Hate. AA."

While her alcoholic heroin addict ex-husband had been in AA, his sponsor had insisted that she attend meetings too. And while she sat in Alanon meetings her husband sold the furniture to feed his habit. When she confronted him about it, he threw her down the same stairs we'd just ascended. She pointed almost proudly to the areas of her face where she'd had extensive surgery. The rhinoplasty had cost extra. If she ever tracked him down she would round up some of the boys and have the word *Rapist* tattooed on his forehead. It was at this point that she mentioned that her best friend was the president of the Hells Angels in Budapest. I could have used that water now, but I was too afraid to speak. Still recovering from the shock of uncovering an AA member in her own home—on her couch, no less—she seemed now to need reassurance.

"But you *do* have the job?" she asked. I nodded carefully. "And the apartment?" she continued.

The Job? The Apartment? Like two out of three wasn't bad. Like I had lied about everything else. She continued as if none of what she had just said could possibly have any effect on what she was about to say. She wanted, she said, to settle down and have a child. She was ready. Was I ready?

She seemed calmer now that she was talking about her future. She sank back into the couch, revealing a tattooed white star only barely visible against the white skin of her midriff. It was a pentagram. Of course it was.

She would obviously be demonic in bed, but a good fuck was a small reward for what she really wanted. Luminous babies and eternal darkness.

Up until that moment, my natural paranoia had been in a state of calm, gathering facts in a half-awake, half-interested manner. With a jolt, I wondered how I could have missed the certain truth of the situation; she was obviously pregnant, and the plan was to first fuck me and then dupe me into bringing up her pasty progeny as my own.

What the fuck was happening here? Was it the suicidal reindeer? Was this really the best I could conjure from the Internet? I looked down at my feet to find that I was descending the stairs with only slightly more dignity than she had when she'd been thrown down them.

• • • •

"I never got to thank you for all the work. It's going well, isn't it?"

Jonathan, our very British account manager, appeared genuine enough, but a manager's work was never done. He might need me to work late or let him kill an idea he couldn't sell or come in to work on a weekend. This was his way of sounding me out. So when I redirected his gratitude to Silvestro, his eyes narrowed. A creative who didn't glawm at easy praise was something to be wary of. Did I know something he didn't? Was this campaign about to be received less favorably than he'd been led to believe?

The preliminary research results indicated that *The Life Less Driven* was a winner. It had already tested through the roof in London, Berlin, Los Angeles, and New York. The idea was simple. Demonstrate the safety of the cars by filming cinema-verité-style films showing driver and passenger conversing freely. Real conversations about real subjects. In real time. The more intoxicating the conversation, the safer the car. The client loved it, since the car was in every single shot, and creatives aspired to it, because the conversations were real. It went beyond advertising. Thirty-second commercials cut from the filmed footage would show a link where the full-length films could be watched at leisure.

It was reality with a logo.

In an all-staff email, Christoph, our German producer, had referred to it as the *Irishman's* campaign. He would never have made an announcement like this if Silvestro hadn't already sanctioned it. My first impulse was to tell everyone I had nothing to do with it, but if the creative director wanted it said that I'd had a hand in this campaign, then who was I to object? Maybe it was his generous gesture of welcome? His way of including me. I also had to tread carefully, since my visa situation had become extremely delicate. The lawyer was now saying my "little hiccup" at the Canadian border could effectively halt my application for a green card. And if my application was halted—well, there was a very real danger I might not work in the United States again. So this was not the time to distance myself from a potentially award-winning campaign. And anyway, hadn't I perpetrated enough good work of my own over the years to piggyback just this once?

Across the room Lucien sat ramrod straight in his chair, expressionless, as he watched me carefully. Without taking those button-black eyes from mine, he began typing so fast that at first I thought he was joking. The screen in front of him was as indecipherable as he was. Macro enlargements of halftone photography woven into layers of transparent type, ground up against jagged slabs of flat black and white. All strangely haphazard and definitely noncommercial. It was like an aerial view of some unforgiving alien landscape, impenetrably obscure, airless and unwelcoming. It was obvious from even a distance that this wasn't agency work. It soon became clear from the galleys and layouts strewn over every available surface of the three-story canal house that Lucien's book of black-and-white photography (mostly black) would soon be published, thanks to agency funds set aside by Silvestro. It would be his reward for past services, and as far as I could tell, it was the only reason he tolerated any of us at all.

What I didn't know was that he had already resigned. As soon as his published books were delivered, he would be gone. Was it just coincidence that I should end up in Amsterdam just as he was leaving? It might have been my all-too-familiar paranoia, but a scenario began to emerge that seemed to explain everything. Maybe Andy had intentionally orchestrated the shoot in Canada, knowing that my visa was up for renewal. He wasn't exactly pleased when he caught me printing out my book, and even less so when I made that comment in the toilet. And with Lucien leaving, they needed someone to help Silvestro. It made sense. As my creative director, Andy could have easily found out the status of my work visa. He could get rid of me and find a use for me at the same time.

If this was true, then I might have to start learning Dutch in earnest. I had learned a few phrases just to appear interested, but I was beginning to see it was the only language I'd ever encountered that could render a beautiful girl ugly just by speaking it. The problem lay in the pronunciation of the letter *G*. The harsher it sounded, the more aristocratic the speech was perceived to be. It was the sort of sound a reasonable man would be forgiven for making after realizing he might have to live in the Netherlands.

A, B, C, D, E, F, Gechchhh . . .

PIPPA

Pippa was an upper-class British girl whose idea of slumming it was to fuck someone like me. She was a fat little fucker, but her accent and demeanor seemed to indicate otherwise. As if actual body fat was something only the lower classes suffered from. Daddy, who she referred to without irony as being an earl, would no doubt be suitably livid when she implied between the Dover sole and the gooseberry fool that she'd bedded a Paddy. I probably made as much money if not more than he did, but I wanted her to see me as a bohemian writer—mostly because I wanted to believe it myself. She drove a little MG sports car that she constantly felt the need to apologize for. In a faraway voice she said I looked like a Labrador, and I somehow knew by this that we were going to have sex. When she took her clothes off, she expanded like dough, and at one point I inserted myself into what I hoped was her pussy, but I had a very real fear that it might be a sweaty fold in her lower belly. I had to close my eyes in order to give the impression I was enjoying the sensation, but she wasn't having it.

"Open your eyes, would you?"

The nubile girls I had conjured in my mind exploded and I suddenly became a sexual plate spinner, trying to keep her nipples erect so that at least I could tell what was tit and what was not. When she got on top of me, I had to suppress an urge to fight. I was beginning to doubt if I could actually orgasm under all that heaving girl-flesh, until she had the decency to reach down and insert one of her fat fingers in my butthole.

I came immediately.

Flushed with relief, I turned to her, grateful that I'd never have to see her again

"I felt something in there," she whispered. "You might want to have it looked at."

The hard-won swirl of endorphins soured inside me.

● ● ● ●

"Apple-sichk, fuchk the duchk in the muchk?"

The receptionist obviously thought I was Dutch.

"I have an appointment with Dr. Van Amersvoort," I explained.

"I'll tell him you're here."

It would seem silly later—childish, even—but the thought that I was going to die from stress-induced cancer of the colon had for the two preceding weeks occupied the width and breath of my being. Advertising had killed me. Pippa's postcoital concern merely confirmed what I had already feared. I'd die elegantly in nearby France while my medical insurance was still eligible. At least I wouldn't have to be insulted by spoken Dutch ever again. But my almost comforting death wish was short-lived when, after administering a gentle lunchtime probing to my virgin sphincter, the doctor declared me benign. I felt relief and then joy. And then relief again. It occurred to me that I had been at least as frightened of getting an erection as a bad diagnosis. You could say I got the all clear in more than one sense.

Mind you, he was an ugly fucker.

Open on an over-the-shoulder-shot of me writing on my laptop. The camera zooms in on the screen until we are looking at what appears to be an extreme close-up of two equal-sized dots positioned one above the other. It's a colon.

:

Voice-over: "Getting checked early can seriously increase your chances of survival." The camera finds and settles into the next extreme close-up—this time, one dot positioned over a comma. A Semicolon.

;

Voice-over: "Getting checked when the disease has already set in can prove more difficult to treat." The next frame shows only one solitary dot. A Period.

.

Voice-over: "Get checked early for colon cancer before it's too late." Issued by the Center for Cancer Research.

VALERIYA

With Silvestro, Christoph, and Jonathan away in Reykjavík shooting the first installment of *The Life Less Driven,* I was left to look after the agency. It was the first of five more shoots that would follow in Hong Kong, Berlin, Lisbon, and Rome. Silvestro had offered me the chance to go instead of him, but it was wrapped in an unspoken expectation that I should stay. It was pure diplomacy. Olaffson had been brave enough to sign off on a Pan-European campaign that had no script, but Silvestro wasn't going to tempt fate by appointing a supervisor who couldn't even remember to bring the proper travel documents to his last shoot. I knew this and Silvestro knew this. But it needed to look like my decision because this was supposedly my campaign.

Pure politics.

And anyway I had far more important issues on my mind. A date with the beautiful Valeriya.

After a giggly visit to the Rijksmuseum, where I jumped out from behind statues like a child surprising his mother, Valeriya opened her lovely full mouth, began to talk, and changed everything. We were sitting in the café downstairs and she was telling me about her many trips to Florence while at the same time sympathizing with me for never having been. She teased me that I couldn't call myself a writer until I had visited Florence at least once.

She went on to say that she would have gone there even more often if the choice had been hers to make, "but that's what life is like when you're . . ."

This is where I experienced what Hitchcock liked to call a *reverse smile*: the sudden removal of a wide beaming smile in reaction to a negative event.

He would have loved the effect on my face on hearing the word *married*. I felt sick and tricked because then and there I realized I had been effortlessly manipulated into wanting her more than I actually did.

The options on datemedotcom profile settings were *Single, Separated,* or *Divorced.* She had selected *Single.* The person sitting opposite me suddenly seemed secondhand, used even. *Of course you're married,* my expression tried to say. Isn't everyone?

I tried to display nonchalance. It would buy me some time to think. Maybe this kind of behavior was standard online. And maybe, just maybe, my instinctual knee-jerk response of *you fucking lying cunt* didn't apply. At least not yet. Then it occurred to me that if she had lied to me, it meant I didn't need to be so respectful anymore. I had spent hours between dates daydreaming about us making love, but now I just wanted to fuck her. And soon, before I found out something else I didn't want to hear. I suggested we drop by my place for dessert, and when she agreed, I thought even less of her.

She paused at the threshold to my apartment as if there was a chance she might not enter, but I took this to be just another lie, assuming she was playing the part of a timid girl so I could feel more powerful. So be it. I pushed the door open, and before she had fully entered, I had peeled away her coat and blouse in one. Her nipples seemed strangely sunken like those of an older woman, but otherwise she was a like a fucking movie star.

"You're like a fucking movie star," I said.

Her long, slim girlish legs shivered apart under my touch and I licked her out and she gave me a sloppy, slippery blow job. She'd been very sneaky about not telling me she was married. In fact she was *still* married. We were committing adultery. Or at least she was. I wanted to ask if she had really been a gymnast or if that was a lie too? I couldn't be sure what was true and what wasn't. To confuse matters even more, the sex was beautiful and loving and dirty all at the same time. She was married. So what? As she teased the tip of my cock with the tip of her tongue, I didn't care if she turned out to be a man. She had a great energy and was cheerful and full of life and laughter and her pussy was the most beautiful I had ever seen in real life. It was so perfectly symmetrical I dubbed it pussuq. She stretched her foot down to stroke my dick as I lapped at her. Was this a trick she used on her husband? Of course it was. I could have stayed down there all day. There was never any need to explain anything to Valeriya. She intuitively understood. At one point I sat with my pants around my knees, half crouched to absorb the shocks as she smashed her pussuq down onto my cock like she was trying to kill something. As she began to exhaust herself on my midriff, I gathered her to me and waddled ankle-panted across the floor and laid her down so I could feast on her. But I wasn't allowed. Springing back up, she bid me kneel and immediately

93

began pummeling me mercilessly with spat-on hands like some sexual laborer.

"Come on, give it to me." It was as if I was withholding her property.

Until then I felt it would be rude to unload the contents of my loins at a girl, but from the look on this girl's face, it began to look like it might be insulting not to. Three white arcs loosed themselves into the void between us. The first two disappeared out of view, but the last clung like a smile to her heaving breasts. I bayed like a dog at an imaginary moon and we hugged for so long after coming I felt like we'd been stirred together like milk into tea. No sugar. And because she was unavailable, it was okay to fall in love with her.

"Come on, be honest. If you were a girl, wouldn't you be a slut?"

The question didn't seem fair because everyone knew girls just didn't think like that. Here was a girl—a beautiful girl—asking me a question that demanded the reorganization of everything I'd ever thought about women. I was suddenly seized with a desire not so much to have her but to *be* her. I was jealous of her freedom. Her power. A great-looking girl could fuck anyone she wanted. Surely such power was intoxicating.

She was like a guy with a girl's body.

Did every girl think like this, but only Valeriya was willing to admit it? She accused me of analyzing everything and pronounced it *anal-izing*.

I couldn't tell if this was because English was her second language and therefore a coincidence or whether she had effortlessly outpunned me.

Was she fucking with me?

"If you were a girl, wouldn't you be a slut?" She repeated the question as if it was a natural progression from what she had just said, and in the full knowledge that I was defeated, I conceded reluctantly that yes, I would.

"Well, there you go."

She said this like it explained everything, but all it did was confuse me even more. She saw herself as a slut?

She knew how to adapt to her surroundings, that's for sure. This was the classic behavior of abused children. Broken people learn how to keep the peace at the expense of our own needs. We merged into any given situation. When two chameleons successfully take on each other's hues, there is nothing there. I emailed her some contacts in advertising and film production in Amsterdam, and her response pretty much said it all. Especially those last two words.

"I don't know how to thank you. Well, I do, but let's pretend."

ANITA

Anita was a long-waisted Muscovite who worked in IT for an international bank based in The Hague. In the time I knew her, she visibly brightened only twice: once when she swallowed an entire glass of whiskey in one gulp, and once when she talked about her combat training as a child: "I am proficient with a Kalashnikov."

I had hopes for some heavy petting and a handful of ass in preparation for the "full deal," which I wanted to suggest would be the following Saturday. When she first turned up, there was a tall, good-looking guy walking behind her, so I assumed they were a couple. But just as I was eyeing her up, thinking *She's not bad,* she broke away from him and stood there in front of me. I was too afraid to stand up in case I came up only to her shoulder. She was tall but surmountable. I flattered myself with thoughts of her expression and imagined it indicated an approval of what she saw too. This was always a tricky moment. Great care had to be taken to hold a poker face, keeping your true feelings of nervousness or disappointment or even glee under wraps. This first date was an audition of sorts, although in a real audition, the actor has a character and script to hide behind. This was two people willfully partic-ipating in an artificially arranged attempt at falling in love.

If you allowed disappointment to creep into your face, you immediately made yourself uglier, thereby inciting an expression in her face that lessened the chances of her look-ing her best, which in turn contributed to a general sense of insecurity.

Hence our crazy smiles.

Her linen trousers were virtually transparent and her tits were perky, just the way I liked them. She seemed to be made up of right angles. All in all, very Slavic. After finishing our meal, we headed to the bar for a drink. She asked me what whiskey I would recommend as a former alcoholic. Without hesitation, I ordered a Jameson's for her. I had become her sommelier. More than once, she started to reach for the glass and stopped herself. It was the sort of reach that uninterrupted would have resulted in her gulping the entire glass down, thereby requiring another to be ordered. I recognized this muffled yearning only too well. She would down it if I wasn't there watching her. And it. The injustice of a whiskey in front of you instead of inside you.

Anything Dutch bored her. We had that much in common. By then I was looking at her the same way she was looking at her glass. She hated Holland but couldn't leave. She said her friends considered her a pain in the ass after she'd had a few drinks.

"In that case, you can count me among your friends," I said.

She smiled at this as if I had just paid her a compliment, and who knows, maybe I had.

"You should take your hand away from your mouth when you talk. It makes you look dishonest," she said.

I could see how she could be a real bitch. But I wouldn't let her get to me. She certainly liked her booze. Three glasses of wine the first night, and this time the subject came up, as it always did.

"Do you have many friends who drink?"

97

I put my hand in front of my mouth.

"Yes," I said.

She laughed reluctantly and that was that.

When we met the next night she wasn't drinking because she was afraid of making me uncomfortable, which had the effect of making her uncomfortable instead. In fact she became frighteningly depressing. Had she necked a couple of whiskeys, I would have been the one exhaling in relief. The less she drank, the less attractive she became in all her wallowing. We cowered in some god-awful seaside restaurant that looked like it might have been on the shores of the Styx, and wordlessly stared out the window as angry white-knuckled waves repeatedly tried to grip the mainland and drag it under.

I tried heroically to keep things light.

"So how was your day?"

"I'm not in a cheerful mood."

"Oh, I'm sorry to hear that. Is it because of work?"

"I just heard that my friend has cancer."

I was sorry to hear that too, because now I was going to have to listen to this shit all night. Cancer, the alcoholic's friend. Nobody could laugh when cancer was in the room.

It must have been killing her. She was looking for an excuse to drink and she even had a good one, but I was still sitting there in front of her—the insistently sober alcoholic.

At the end of the evening I tried to kiss her more from duty than desire, but she almost snapped her neck pulling away. It would have been more depressing if I hadn't even tried. Was there such a thing as a nice pretty girl who wasn't divorced, married, or fucking crazy? Was that possible? On closer inspection, Anita was a communist-built structure teetering on the brink of collapse. I still wanted to at least see her naked.

"Wow."

"Wow? What does this mean? *Wow?*"

"The passion," I said.

"I'm deciding if I should go or stay."

I had come all the way to The Hague to hear this.

"And you're short," she added. It was with a smile, but she said it.

"It doesn't matter when you're lying down."

"You're not lying down *all* the time."

I wanted to tell her to go fuck herself, but I'd come all the way here and I felt I was owed something. Something I'd have to wait to get.

"You could be a sweet guy, but you hide behind the jokes," she said at last.

Then she told me she was still married, but I hardly even heard her. When Valeriya told me the same thing, I nearly broke in half. Anita and her husband of seven years had lived in a very respectable neighborhood in the Hague. I was suddenly thinking about Valeriya. I couldn't comprehend how she had become so deeply embedded in my being. Like an arrow that hurts less if it is allowed to remain in place.

Anita was almost waving as she tried to get my attention. She invited me back to a depressingly large, mostly white apartment. Didn't she say she had a husband somewhere? Was this where she took her online dates? Would the husband walk in any second? The moment we got inside, she turned around and kissed me. I had no idea she would be so feminine and gentle under all that Slavic frost. We ripped at our clothes as if they had become poisonous. Naked and with her hair down around those slender shoulders, she became so much nicer. Sweet, even.

She whispered to me as I fucked her.

"I love eeet . . . yessss, oh baby . . . ohhhhh, nice . . . nail me!"

Nail me?

She got on top and let her hair fall over me like darkness.

I laughed out loud when she orgasmed because the sounds she made were so girlish and innocent, I just assumed she was faking it. But then I saw the telltale red patches on her neck and chest like embarrassment. With her taut stomach still shivering against mine and my cock still hard inside her, I began to feel something other than just lust for her.

It was gratitude.

The sort of gratitude you feel for someone who has done you a great kindness. There was a selflessness about her in that moment that endeared me to her. I had never made a girl come solely from fucking before. And the fact that I hadn't come yet merely confirmed my status as stud. I'd give her a rest before going again. Lying there beneath her limp, perspiring body, with her hair spilling across my face, I began to talk about, of all people, Valeriya. How she had lied to me. How I was better off without her. How she saw herself as a slut. I couldn't stop. I even mentioned the magical lure of the pussuq.

And because I felt I was at least being listened to, I began to talk about Yvette. How she had insisted I join her in a therapy session with her psychiatrist. The gray-haired, lesbian-looking woman who had heard so much about me (all bad) had decided it was time she met me. Fifteen seconds after being introduced, she asked me the one question I didn't want to be asked by anyone anywhere ever: "Do you love her?" My silence was more eloquent than any answer I could select. Anita continued to make soothing sounds of encouragement. She was hearing my confession, making me truly hers to inhabit. How girlish she had turned out to be after all. A minute passed before I realized she was snoring. She had fucked me and fallen asleep.

REBECCA

Rebecca's profile picture showed her straining against the confines of a skintight minidress in mid-conversation at a party. The faceless silhouetted male with whom she chatted was obviously for presentation purposes only. *Look at my scorching-hot body.* This was how she wanted to be seen on a dating site. In another picture, a close-up of her face, she looked like the aging mother of the party girl.

Her aristocratic accent confirmed she had spent her childhood in Oxford. Following her parents' death in a tragic auto accident, Rebecca was sent to live with her uncle, a former Oxford professor who had moved to Amsterdam after an incident with one of his students. He would turn out to be her first sexual experience when he made her come with his fingers. She was fifteen.

I had by now realized that I could use my abuse as a sort of twisted method of getting sex and sexuality into a conversation. Because I had introduced the idea of using a safety pin to lock my predator out, she felt comfortable enough to confess some experiences of her own.

"So he abused you?" I ventured.

"Yes, I suppose so, but he didn't go all the way. I mean, he didn't actually have sex with me."

I was reminded of how I had defended Brother Ollie, because in defending him I could convince myself that I had actually *wanted* my balls fondled by a clergyman. She was astonishingly generous with her sexual musings. In fact I got the impression she was relieved to talk to someone about it all. Relieved and maybe even a little turned on. It was sad to think of all that sexuality dammed up inside the conservative life of a geography teacher in Amsterdam. She looked like she was holding her breath permanently. But after one kiss, Agatha Christie became Julie Christie, and yes, she had the accent to match. You need six hundred years of British op-pression stored away in your DNA to appreciate the satisfac-tion of thrusting your undeserving Irish cock into a mouth that has just finished saying, "Darling, I've been frightfully busy today."

Fucking her took on political status.

"This is for the Famine, and this is for Bloody Sunday, now turn over, this is for Maggie Thatcher. And this? This is for Princess Dian-aaaaaaggggh."

On rain-soaked Mondays, which were indistinguish-able from any other day of the week in the Netherlands, she cheered herself up by appearing in front of her class wearing a light gray one-piece boilersuit that showed off her lithe body to full effect.

When she turned to write on the chalkboard, the class fell silent. For most teachers it was the other way around. It was an honor, she said, to be part of their sexual awakening.

She intentionally made spelling mistakes at the chalk-board, knowing full well that she would first need to bend and reach for the eraser before shaking herself vigorously as she scrubbed the word away. She delighted in the idea of these boys pummeling themselves at home under the blan-kets with the image of her superb ass coaxing them out of puberty.

And she loved to suck me off. It was the first thing she'd do. I began to think her uncle had taught her well. She was so good at it only because she enjoyed it so much.

103

I felt seriously twisted that this thought should even occur to me, and if I had any sort of decency, my cock would have softened and we would have stopped. But it didn't. If anything, the idea that fifteen years later I should benefit from the sexual teachings of an Oxford don surged into my balls, up the length of my undeserving Irish cock and down her gulping, well-spoken throat. And the moment just before she reached her own orgasm she would look at me as if she'd just been grossly insulted. Like she was being overtaken not by ecstasy but by a shuddering exhalation of abhorrence. As if all the platitudes and denials burned away, and there beyond the smoke for a split second was the reality.

A Mick was fucking her.

OLGA

"You live a charmed life."

Seeing myself through the jealous eyes of my house-guest felt unexpectedly good.

Tim was only halfway through his first day and he'd already visited the red-light district and two of its prostitutes before we even got back to my place.

Tim was a sexual tourist and my apartment was his base.

As a fellow AA member from Saint Lacroix, I had gotten to know him just enough to invite him to visit me in New York, but he had never taken me up on it because I suppose New York didn't offer the same sexual possibilities as Amsterdam. And what's more, he had supposedly fallen in love with a Russian girl, and so a short layover in Amsterdam seemed to him to be a good idea before continuing on to Moscow. It transpired after only a little questioning that the girl in Moscow whom he now talked about marrying was in fact a self-confessed—I didn't dare say the word in front of him because he was convinced she was his girlfriend—prostitute. Tim was what I imagined a hooker dreamed of.

A constant source of employment.

He talked about asking her to come and live with him in Saint Lacroix. Meanwhile, from among the well-maintained red-lit windows, he selected a rather buxom girl who wouldn't have been my first choice, but it was his money, not mine. While I waited for him outside in the street I noticed a girl in an adjacent window who, when she thought no one was looking, took swigs from a tall glistening black bottle and surreptitiously stroked the white tail of a cat hidden behind her little bed. The tail straightened between her slender fingers like some headless python, or yes, I suppose, a penis. I felt like I was spying on her life between fucks and sucks.

I had already spent more time than I would have liked waiting on the little brown-bricked bridge for Tim and his sex worker to conclude their transaction. Flanked by his luggage, I looked like a newly arrived tourist, and as such, found myself scrutinizing the area as if I had indeed just arrived. I noticed for the first time that the window-shoppers weren't all men. Behind gently embarrassed smiles and bathed momentarily in reflected red fluorescent light, women looking surprisingly comfortable in such a potentially controversial area slowed down as if recognizing something familiar about it all. It was the business of attraction. The Dow Jones of who wanted who. Maybe they were reassured by the fact that if you were alluring enough or just present enough (some of the prostitutes were unashamedly ugly), you too would eventually attract your man. Here sexual attraction was reduced to its barest necessities. There was no literature, no sonnets, just naked sexual honesty. The yearning of organs for organs chaperoned by their owners. There was something maddeningly straightforward about it. It was all so practical. So very Dutch.

You want sex. We have it.

Tim finally emerged from the one-girl brothel without even a trace of a smile.

He preferred his women not to make sound at all.

"I appreciate it if they just stay quiet. I always tell them this in advance. If they charge one-fifty, I'll put three hundred down so I have some room for maneuver."

I was impressed by this no-nonsense, albeit paradoxical approach. I would need to believe they wanted me for the encounter to have any value. After all, wasn't this what was on sale? The illusion that a beautiful young woman was aroused by me. But by letting them know he wasn't interested in their performance, Tim held control of the situation. And control was the real commodity here. You were absolved of the pressure to figure out if a woman *actually* wanted you. Tim already knew they didn't mean it, so why should he have to suffer their bad acting? He said he couldn't come with the buxom hooker because she spoke to him, and in doing so, she broke the sexual equivalent of the fourth wall.

"Have you been smokink maruijana?" He mimicked her. "You only get ze one position," and when he couldn't come, "Maybe you should cut it off, ja?"

He picked up his bag with the airport tags still attached and we were about to head back to my place when he noticed the girl with the Liebfraumilch beckoning and gesturing toward us. Even though she gyrated amateurishly and giggled unconvincingly, I felt a stirring.

Tim didn't know that she was beckoning at me. Or maybe he did. Either way he didn't care. I tried to find some way to claim her as my own. I'd seen her first.

Surely he wasn't about to just go and fuck her so soon after the last one? She was a prostitute and as such she was only doing what a prostitute does. She was standing there nearly naked in a window coming on to men for money. Legally. It was a strange sensation. As if she was just performing in three dimensions what we all knew but were too afraid or too ashamed to talk about. That men wanted sex and women wanted security. And yes, of course I wanted her, but I couldn't bring myself to pay for a woman like a cut of meat from a butcher. And my poor little ego couldn't handle the notion that any guy with the correct amount of cash would fill this slot. Literally.

She had winked at me while I waited for Tim and now she was going to fuck him? Tim dropped his bag again and looked at me. He could see something was going on between the girl and me.

"I won't be long," he said.

The uninvited heat of jealousy invaded my thoughts and my initial, almost naive sexual fervor for the girl in the window dissolved first into disgust at her, then hatred for him, and finally anger at myself. What the fuck was I doing standing there waiting for this asshole to get his rocks off? With a whore. Had the filthy little cunt noticed something competitive between Tim and I and capitalized on it? She had seen him arrive and watched me wait for him. And this was business, after all. She was after a sale. How had I been tricked into this? After what seemed like an eternity, Tim reappeared, and I searched his face for some sign of pleasure or relief or shame or spite.

"I fucked her in the ass," he said.

I felt filthy. I was as jealous and enraged as if he had fucked my girlfriend. I felt wronged, but what could I say? It disgusted me to think that by being there I had inadvertently added to his pleasure. There was no conceivable way to justify what I was feeling, which made the feeling even more dangerous. I couldn't berate Tim for fucking this beautiful young girl any more than I could if he had rented a rowboat. But why did I feel so enraged? So betrayed? So . . . hurt? I was jealous that Tim had fucked a prostitute.

I called my sponsor and he suggested that I tell Tim he should get a hotel room. So this was what I did. He wasn't even surprised when I told him that I disagreed with what he was doing and that I felt it was not sober behavior. It was as if he wanted me to throw him out so that he could think even less of himself than he already did.

"Oh, by the way," he said before he left, "her name is Olga."

Open on a shot of me in Albert Heijn Supermarket.

I take out my credit card and swipe it in the self-service console. A green light flickers and we hear an automated voice: "Astobuleef." In subtitles we see the translation: "Thank you." Bagged groceries are lowered into my cart and I wheel them away. Cut to another scene, this time I'm buying some new clothes and swiping my credit card as the same greeting appears in a friendly flashing typeface. "Astobuleef" (Thank you). I exit the store with my shopping bags. Cut to an interior of my apartment. I'm wearing the clothes I bought earlier and I've prepared a beautiful dinner for two with the groceries. The doorbell sounds, and after one last look at the table to make sure everything is in place, I open the door to reveal a stunningly beautiful young girl standing in the doorway. Before she enters the apartment, she asks me for my credit card. Taking it, she reaches up

under her skirt and appears to insert it between her legs. She
stands motionless for a second, smiling at me as if waiting
for the result, and then her eyes widen and a huge seduc-
tive smile spreads across her face. "Astobuleef," she says
seductively, and steps into the apartment. A title appears on
screen: "God is good but business is better." Issued by the
Dutch Institute of Commerce.

PAMELA

"Tell me he's going with you, Jonathan, you can't not
bring him."

In taking up my cause like this, my newly employed assistant Pamela made it seem like Jonathan hadn't already decided to invite me to the awards ceremony, when for all any
of us knew, he might have come upstairs to do exactly that.

She had employed such a strategy, I imagined, since it
would seem like she was fighting in my corner while getting
rid of me at the same time. She had been hired when Lucien
left because even though he and I were both art directors, I
had none of his computer skills. Pamela was not an art director, but she was fluent in Photoshop, InDesign, After Effects,
and many other programs I hadn't even heard of. Also recommending her for the job, as far as I was concerned, was
the fact that there was no danger of anything even vaguely
sexual ever transpiring between us, since she had difficulty
squeezing herself in, and extricating herself from, between
the armrests of a normal-sized chair. This seemed to suggest

that my superiors knew more about my proclivities than I realized.

Her substantial presence made mine even less relevant. She could easily make all the adaptations necessary for the print ads and posters, which was all that was left to do now that *The Life Less Driven* was running across Europe. In fact there was now no need at all for me to be in Amsterdam apart from the fact that I had been *deported*. This was the term being used in agency emails to describe my situation. But Pamela was no mere technician; she was also the self-appointed curator of the Agency Celebrity Phone List.

Hilarious, if (like Silvestro) you resembled the classic Italian film star Marcello Mastroianni, or (like Christoph) you were often mistaken for the Dutch footballer Sven van Beek. The Agency Celebrity Phone List sat laminated on every desk, by every phone, so that every photographer, illustrator, visiting client, or pizza delivery guy saw your name and extension under an image of Uncle Fester.

Was this Pamela's revenge on me for making her work so late and so often while I rummaged around online looking for women? (I was convinced she checked my "recent history.") Seeing the trauma in my face the first day the list appeared, and perhaps fearing retribution in the form of even longer hours, she confessed. "Silvestro said to find a picture of Uncle Fester. I didn't know what it was for."

I let her off light. After all, her name appeared under a picture of Princess Fiona, Shrek's wife.

But Jonathan (Colin Firth) responded to her beseeching with a gracious smile and handed me a large manila envelope full of mail diverted from the New York office.

I knew without opening it that it contained director's showreels and photographer's brochures begging me for possible employment. Dropping off the envelope was probably the only reason he had stopped by, but now that Pamela had shamed him into it, he did indeed invite me to join Silvestro, Christoph, and himself for a weekend in Cannes for the Cannes Lions advertising awards, and I of course accepted graciously, because what kind of a crazy bastard would refuse an all-expenses-paid trip to the South of France?

They presented an agency with a Titanium Award only when something was so fabulous they felt it needed a special category to itself. Only four of them had been awarded since the birth of the Cannes Lions festival in 1964. Apparently *The Life Less Driven* fell under just such a category. I wanted to call someone and share the news, but there was no one. I thought of Rebecca, but what was the point? She'd be moving to Berlin in a few weeks and she'd have a new guy within the month. My mother wouldn't even understand, and even if she did, all she'd want to hear was whether there was some money in it for her. My sponsor? He'd feel obliged to congratulate me, but so what? Congratulations and don't forget to share your gratitude at a meeting—oh, and no booze.

The ceremony wasn't until eight PM the following Saturday, so we could have easily gotten an afternoon flight but because Jonathan wanted to get away from his children—so many, so loud; I had to get up at six on a Saturday morning to meet the flight he'd booked for us. He could see I wasn't very happy about it.

"You'll thank me later when we have a nice dinner."

He smelled like he was still drunk from the night before. I couldn't summon even token excitement at the prospect of receiving the equivalent of an Oscar for a campaign I'd had nothing to do with. We hadn't even taken off yet and I couldn't wait to get back. Suffice it to say, I am not a morning person.

By the time we got on the stage that night after an eternity of delayed flights and a torturously slow cab ride from the airport, I felt like I'd been outmaneuvered yet again. I'd only just managed to get into the shitty little hotel room when I heard Jonathan shouting from the street that we were late, so I hurriedly changed into my evening wear. We met in the hotel, where I was confronted by triplets. Silvestro, Christoph, and Jonathan all wore simple white shirts and dark identical comfortable jeans. Had they agreed on what to wear? They exuded the demeanor of talented people accustomed to the logistics of receiving awards. While their light-colored clothes deflected the heat of the spotlights, I stood there staring at the other three in consternation. In my black cowboy shirt, black jeans, and crepe-soled brothel creepers, I looked like a guy who had no connection with the other three. I had become the American who didn't get it.

The camera flashes were blinding. I stood rigidly up on the stage. The area around my feet was scratched and scuffed and over-lit and dirty. There was dandruff on the photographer and feedback from the microphones. The curtain was frayed and the music was canned, the applause reluctant, the podium perspex. This was the view from the top?

The sonic boom as reality collides with the billboard's promise.

LIESBETH

Later, Silvestro, Christoph, and Jonathan held court in a booth at the Noisette d'Or, and sitting next to Silvestro was a girl so beautiful she essentially rendered him invisible. She was so insultingly beautiful, I felt an inexplicable urge to retaliate at something or someone.

I was invited to sit down and watch them all get drunk.

"Hi, I'm Liesbeth. I don't think we've met?"

Liesbeth, I decided, had developed an expression of perpetual severity so that mortal men might be spared the full brunt of her allure. So flattering was her beauty in its relaxed state that even the weakest smile ignited fantasies. When she told the table she and her boyfriend had bought a place in Amsterdam and then split up, every face brightened involuntarily and then dampened comically. She was, after all, Silvestro's girl now. After a few drinks, Jonathan seemed to have developed a maddening itch on his upper arm that required him to push back the sleeve of a T-shirt that ordinarily concealed his Maori-style tattoo from clients. Christoph, already quite drunk, continuously took pictures of himself and whoever else was nearby so that presumably the following morning, he could consult the digital oracle for clues as to what had happened the night before. His camera turned blackouts into brownouts. There was an ad for cameras in there somewhere. Meanwhile, I tried very hard not to get caught ogling the upturned braless breasts of his unbearably beautiful neighbor while Silvestro somehow managed, in spite of her protestations and gentle arm slaps, to finish a story about Leonardo DiCaprio hitting on her in a club in New York. The punch line, it turned out, was that she didn't even know who he was.

Liesbeth rolled her eyes as if to say *Silvestro is such a charming liar,* but behind this mock mortification, her eyes twinkled with glee.

I decided my role for the evening was to be impressed. Oh, how wonderful it all was. How fortunate to be at the winning table, where Titanium, Gold, and Silver Lions sat like ornaments on the linen. Oh, thank you all for allowing me a seat at your table. And for a desk in your agency. I kept one hand on the water glass, making sure it didn't get filled with wine. People were very generous with booze when they weren't paying for it.

Liesbeth turned toward me, looking very serious.

"Do you mind people drinking around you?"

"No, it doesn't bother me."

"Silvestro says you don't drink at all?"

"No."

"Nothing?"

"No."

"Ever?"

"No."

"Not even at Christmas?"

"No."

"No joints either?"

"No."

"You don't do *anything*?"

I'd already said it too many times but there was no other word for it.

"No."

This was not the answer she wanted, and now she wrinkled her pretty brow. I felt like I'd ruined the mood and I was ready to change the subject. Jonathan was looking interested in my direction. Christoph had put away his phone and Silvestro was sitting back in his chair, the better to regard my discomfort. I was, after all, the only one at the table who wasn't on the brink of getting absolutely fucking sloshed. It seemed only fair that I should explain myself. I tried to think of a way to change the subject. The awards. The weather. The French. Her bracelet. Did she get it locally? Your bracelet, I like your bracelet.

"But don't you ever feel the need"—she paused here, selecting and discarding phrases—"to escape yourself?"

It was a revealing question. It told me that she considered it normal to want to escape herself. It was as if I'd caught a glimpse of her on the toilet. The thing now was not to be critical of her. Or the rest of the table.

A silence had descended. An answer was expected.

"Well," I said, now addressing the entire table, "I suppose I try to make myself more inhabitable."

Was *inhabitable* even a word?

Fuck it, she was a foreigner.

I hadn't noticed until that moment that she was smoking a joint so well rolled it looked like a cigarette, and the glass of white wine on the linen in front of her was so full it might have been water. Inhaling from the joint, she raised her glass, sipped, swallowed, and regarded me anew. I didn't see her exhale.

"I like your bracelet," I said quickly.

This somehow signaled the all clear, and the conversation resumed around the table. I tried not to look too relieved. Silvestro was still looking at me.

"I hear you've written a book."

It was true that during a quiet moment before we sat down to dinner I had mentioned to Christoph that I'd written something, but only because he'd asked me, and I hadn't said it was a book. I said I'd written *something* and that I wasn't even sure what it was. Christoph ap-

117

peared unsurprised, but then he was a producer—that was his job.

It occurred to me afterward that the file containing my book was accessible on the agency's shared network, so it was possible Christoph had already noticed it there before I told him about it that evening. For all I knew, he might have even read it. Either way, he'd obviously mentioned it to Silvestro, who, despite Lucien's best efforts to deplete it, still had money left in the project's slush fund. As he continued talking, I didn't hear, so much as see, Silvestro's mouth open and close in apparent slo-mo around words that seemed to suggest that he might like to publish this so-called book of mine. He would need to read it first, of course, and I would need to continue putting effort into the agency in the meantime, but maybe I could send him the file so he could get an idea of what it was about? He couldn't risk the possibility that I might put less energy into the agency than I had done recently, and publishing my book would keep me motivated and give me a reason not leave them all in the shit. I was, after all, at that point the only one beside Pamela who knew where all the files could be found, and what would happen if she were to quit? I nearly cried when I heard him say the word *publish,* because even though it was like a dream coming true, it was cheapened by the fact that in doing so I might be strengthening my connections to the advertising business when my intention had been to write a book that did the opposite.

"Can I think about it?"

"Yes, of course, take your time. No rush."

He of all people understood the need to pretend to think about it.

Open on a wide shot of me checking into a tiny little cheap hotel on a back street in Cannes. A shrunken old man in the tiny reception area hands me a key. Cut to inside the room as I enter and look around. It'll do. Shrugging my bags to the floor, I make my way straight to the bathroom, and after a few moments, we hear two distinct, unmistakable plops. There is a gurgling sound, but the cistern seems to be faulty. I try flushing again. Nothing. I pick up the phone, and when the old man at the front desk answers, I say in my very best French: "Monsieur, la toilette ne marche pas."

There is silence. The old man doesn't understand.

"Toilet. Not. Work," I say again.

Cut to the wizened old man in reception as he repeats the phrase: "Toleet. Non. Quoi?"

Cut back to me holding a burning match to dispel the odor. I try once more to flush the toilet, but with no success. There is a quiet knock on the door, and when I open it, there is a beautiful young girl standing there in an apron. She smiles professionally.

"Il y a un problème, monsieur?"

She might be the old man's daughter or granddaughter or niece.

119

"Ah yes, over here." She follows me to the bathroom.

I nod at the toilet bowl and she looks away, horrified. I frantically wave at her to regain her attention and to effectively wipe away the memory of what she's just seen. I behave now like we're starting all over again. I raise my index finger in front of her face. I hold it there hypnotically before theatrically motioning my hand toward the flush handle and slowly, as if demonstrating to a child, I push it downward. The toilet flushes perfectly. I stare at the toilet bowl in disbelief. The girl starts to cry. My mouth opens as I try to find some way to explain.

LearnNewLanguagesDotcom

LUISA

The fact that MANG094's picture was fuzzy would normally have served as a warning, but I had nothing better to do that Sunday evening after returning from Cannes, and meeting her for a coffee would kill an hour or two before dinner. On the way there I found myself walking behind a small girl with a world-class ass and I remember worrying that I'd be late if I didn't overtake her. But I couldn't bear to leave that ass behind. I looked ahead to the Anne Frank Huis, where we had arranged to meet, but apart from the ever-present well-curated queue of tourists, I saw no one. The little girl in front of me stopped abruptly and took out her cell phone. I could see now that her face was pitted and pocked and not at all attractive and certainly not as young as

I had first assumed. My phone rang, and when she heard it, she looked up and smiled.

"Hi, I'm Luisa."

She was Argentinian. They value an ass down there. I guessed she must have been in her early forties, but she might have been older. She never told me her age and seemed to delight in the idea that I couldn't guess. She did something indecipherable for a pharmaceutical company in Amsterdam, and as she explained exactly what this entailed, I pretended to understand completely. She referred to her daily gym visits as *ass maintenance*. She was out of the country more than she was in it, and when she returned, she always had a new set of lingerie to model for me. She took almost as much pleasure in the beauty of her body as I did. She was addicted to the effect she had on me.

I was a full-length mirror with an erection.

She was so compact and toy-like I could fuck her and fold her away afterward. Her pockmarks blurred together when we kissed and refocused hideously when I pulled back. This drew me closer to her like an exhausted boxer hugging an opponent.

She made frequent references to a breed of ape called the bonobo, who apparently gave one another blow jobs. I couldn't tell if it was a remnant from a prior relationship or whether it was just a cute affectation, but she would actually use the term *bobo* to describe a blow job. As she knelt there in front of me, her face was so firmly attached to my midriff she looked like she had a beard of balls.

Afterward we sat naked looking out on the canals from the window of her apartment. We could see right up the Reguliersgracht. Quite a pretty sight on a clear evening. We ate strawberries and Ben & Jerry's and muesli. It was the perfect relationship for me. Her body was amazing and her face was a built-in get-out clause.

"My doctor thinks it's a mess."

She looked directly at me, making sure I understood. What was a mess? Her face? Her health? What kind of a doctor would describe a patient's health in this way? The Dutch were known for being direct, but this sounded a little harsh.

"So it's a mess," I said and smiled as if this was the cutest thing in the world.

It was a weird moment because by now she was sitting astride me grinning and grinding herself down onto me and I was seconds away from a reignited hard-on. She seemed relieved, somehow. Younger looking. I smiled up at her and then hid in her hair as she began shoving herself back and forth on me.

On my way home, as the effects of two successive orgasms wore off, I realized what her doctor had really said.

"He thinks it's MS."

Multiple sclerosis.

Luisa was worried I'd stop seeing her if I found out. She was right.

•   •   •

The next day it was announced in a group email that Silvestro was leaving. He had accepted a job as editor in chief of *Passione* magazine in Rome. The email made it sound like he would be immediately replaced, but it was just a smoke screen to keep the Olaffson clients from panicking. In fact, the New York office was already dealing with the logistics of closing the place down. Though there was no love lost between Silvestro and the New York office, he didn't want to be sued for leaving their Olaffson client without a creative director in Amsterdam. Publishing my book would at least ensure the semblance of normalcy until the agency closed.

The files were already with the printers when he announced he was leaving, so it was already too late to stop production of my book. Meanwhile, swiveling in his celebrated chair at the helm of a Titanium-winning, almost empty ad agency, I was faced with the most urgent and unexpectedly delightful assignment of my career as an art director. The design of my own book jacket.

I settled on a typographic style that mimicked what a real publisher might do, and after only a few hours working on it, even I could see it was beginning to approach the coast of something that might not get laughed at in a bookshop. It was Pamela's suggestion to apply for a bar code, and again I agreed only because I thought it would make the book more convincing. I sat back relishing the sensation, and something caught my eye.

Between the awards at Cannes and Silvestro's departure, I hadn't had a chance to open the manila envelope that Jonathan had handed me the week before.

Among the glossy enticements to work with the cream of New York's photographers, directors, and stylists was a plain-looking envelope with a government eagle embossed in the right-hand corner. My green card was approved.

Open on a shot of me reading a book. I'm looking rather smug. Panning around the apartment we see unopened cardboard boxes stacked haphazardly. They look like they've just been delivered, and in one opened box we see copies of the same book I'm reading so intently, Diary of an Oxygen Thief *by Anonymous. Suddenly I'm distracted by muffled snippets of a flagrant argument coming from upstairs. Cut to the arguing couple in the apartment above mine. The fact that they are speaking Dutch adds to the aggression of the situation. Translation subtitles appear on the screen.*

"What time do you call this? It's our anniversary, how could you forget?" the girl says.

"I didn't forget, I just bumped into Bob," says the man defensively.

"Bob? Nobody's called Bob anymore."

"Bob. You know Bob, he asked about you."

"I don't care if Robert De Niro asked after me."

She smashes a vase. Cut back to me downstairs as I take out my cell phone.

"Yes, I think maybe you probably can help," I say into the receiver. Cut back upstairs. The girl is shouting now. "What I would like to know is where you've been for the last four hours?"

"Three, actually."

"Four, and you said you went out to get milk."

"I got the milk."

"But I've been cooking all day, it's our anniversary."

Just then, we hear the sound of a doorbell.

"Oh, that might be Bob for you now," she says sarcastically. Opening the door, she is met with a huge bunch of flowers handed to her by a courier. Assuming her boyfriend ordered these beautiful flowers for their anniversary, she throws herself into his arms. Tears of rage become tears of joy as the boyfriend accepts her sensuous kiss of gratitude. Cut back to me downstairs. My smug expression has returned and I settle back into my chair. I am about to resume reading when I hear the loud annoying creak of bedsprings as my upstairs neighbors make love. The plan worked too well.

Tulip Express. Flower Delivery. Amsterdam.

And so it turned out that on that last Friday in February, I alone was summoned to the couches downstairs where the human resources manager, David Long, waited for me—

125

half standing, half sitting, inhaling only when absolutely necessary, as if our office was a quarantined building.

He presented me with a beautifully printed crisp memo announcing the closure of the company that same day. I marveled at the quality of the paper and the opacity of the ink. This certainly hadn't come out of our printer. Within an hour my entry card to the building was canceled. Orchestrating a remote electronic lockout from thousands of miles away was a breeze for our corporation, yet the printer upstairs hadn't worked in all the time I'd been there.

The satellite had embarrassed the mother ship by doing too well. The Amsterdam office wasn't meant to win awards. Our little office was intended as an outpost only. We had exceeded our brief. The Gold, Silver, and Titanium Lions were already on show in a display case in the New York office. Jonathan was offered a position in the new European office they were setting up in London, and he jumped at the opportunity to return home to Blighty. But within two weeks of selling his place in Amsterdam and moving his family back there, he was let go. They had wanted to get him out of his employee-friendly Dutch contract.

But it wasn't all bad news. I received a hundred thousand euros in severance pay.

JANE
"Has Sean Killallon taken out a contract on you yet?"
Jane Duncan, editor of the London media blog/magazine

Ad Vent, had finished reading my newly minted book. One mention in *Ad Vent* would do a lot to get the name out there. But how did she know the fictionalized ad agency in *Diary of an Oxygen Thief* was about Killallon? She knew the ad business better than anyone, but still . . .

"Is it that obvious?"

"Frankly, yes. See page 109."

I ripped open a box, grabbed a book, and, bracing myself, opened it to that page.

". . . done *Killallon a lot of favors.*"

It was nightmarish.

The one word that shouldn't appear anywhere in the book and there it was.

I tried to come to terms with the horror of it. Fighting the feelings would only make them stronger. I had to accept it quickly and then deal with it. How could I have been such an amateur? It was bad enough having typos all the way through, but this was unforgivable. A lawsuit would generate publicity, sure, but not enough to make up for the worry, stress, and legal costs. I had an overwhelming urge to run. Just run. But where?

I was beginning to see what people meant when they said the book was courageous. I didn't like hearing that, because *courageous* meant risky. I suddenly felt like one of my more staid clients who hadn't had the balls to run a cool ad campaign.

Letting that word through was suicide.

I kept returning to the moment I found out like a slo-mo replay of an own goal. Somehow the name of the company got through and it was now printed in thousands of copies.

A glum inevitability descended on me like ash.

I accepted my fate and assumed it into my character. It seemed logical to let the feeling of abject defeat settle inside me, since it would obviously be around for some time. What would prison be like? Would I be expected to suck cocks? I had better get used to the idea. I looked at bananas anew. Would I be expected to swallow?

Yes, I would.

I consulted porn for pointers. If my survival rested on sucking cocks, I would take pride in it. It couldn't really be that bad. I mean, at least I'd still be alive. Sort of. And I could always write about it. If my cellmate let me. I heard about a prisoner who had avoided being raped because he was funny. In prison, humor is as valuable as cigarettes. And everybody knew that a repeatedly raped prisoner didn't tell jokes. Talk about motivation to come up with new material.

Maybe it was a clever attempt by Pamela to undermine me? Could she have been so devilishly clever? It was just a matter of removing the space between the words so that Killallon was rendered invisible to my endless word searches. I had checked and double-checked so many times, but she was the one who sent the final package to the printers, not me. It was surreal to see it there in the finished book.

But on what grounds would they sue me? For not liking them? For defamation? For slander? The Athenaeum Book-shop called and left a message. "It's selling well, we'll take another batch if you have them."

Oh, fuck.

Open on a dizzying over-the-shoulder shot of me stand-ing out on the ledge of a high-rise office building. I look distraught and disheveled. The voice-over sounds like my own thoughts.

"This is where I'm supposed to remind you of all the wonderful things you have to live for, but since it's a little late for that, here's a question for you instead. Are you up high enough? If you jump from this height, you might actu-ally survive, and we don't want that, now do we? Yes, you could always come back and take the disabled elevator to the roof and roll yourself off, but wouldn't it be better to get it right the first time? I think you need a few more floors be-tween the pavement and the possibility of people saying the fucking idiot couldn't even kill himself properly. Come on, the stairs are through here."

This actually makes sense, and as I begin to shuffle back toward the open window, I realize the voice isn't an inner monologue; it's a real person speaking to me from just inside the window. As he helps me inside, I can see he is a calmer, more handsome version of me. He wears exactly the same clothes as I do, but on him they look tailor-made. He is my better self.

As I stand there still staring at him, I am suddenly surrounded by caregivers and paramedics, and wrapped in a blanket before being helped into the elevator. Later, from inside an ambulance I see my twin again as he gets in on the passenger side of a champagne-colored Olaffson parked nearby. Beside him in the driver's seat is a beautiful dark-haired blue-eyed girl. They kiss hello. A wide generous smile spreads across her face when she notices the resemblance between me and my twin, and I can't help feeling I've met her somewhere before, or that we will meet soon. This notion has a calming effect until something occurs to me. I look upward. The camera follows my gaze and we realize the car is parked directly below the window ledge where I threatened to jump. It would have been destroyed when I landed on it. The woman and my better self drive away, smiling happily.

You'll Do Anything to Protect Your Olaffson. And Vice Versa.

BRIDGIT (PART 2)

An apartment in the East Village for nine hundred a month? It was too good to be true. There had to be a catch.

Surely she was setting me up for some terrible revenge. Had I hurt her more than I realized? Poor thing. I had broken her heart, and this was her long-awaited opportunity to avenge herself. She'd stand by as I gave up my place in Amsterdam. She'd even help with my transatlantic move until, on the same day I arrived in New York with as many boxes of my newly published book as the luggage limit allowed, I'd be told there was no apartment. I'd stand there ridiculous, caught between countries, apartments, and cartons of my self-published, semi-fictionalized memoir.

My paranoia suggested this would serve me right for not marrying her. When I finally met her to pick up the keys, she had a baby with her in a huge carriage. I was not expecting this.

"I didn't mention I was married?"

So much for my image of her pining for me in darkened rooms. I peered into the carriage, and from under all manner of expensive-looking blankets and toys emerged a tiny fist like a parody of rebellion. Attached to the fist was an arm, leading up to a shoulder, and finally a head that I could only describe as a bald, blue-eyed miniature version of myself.

Why was she watching my reaction so carefully? Was this in fact *my* baby? Had she gotten pregnant and never told me? I tried to do the math as I smiled and wiggled my fingers in front of . . .

"What's his name?" I was looking for clues.

"Tarquin," she said, enjoying my embarrassment.

"Tarquin. And how old is he now?"

It had been three years since we broke up. Nine months to incubate and . . . oh, Jesus, had she arranged to get me an apartment in her building virtually opposite her own apartment so I could take up my responsibility in parenting our child?

"He's ten months old."

Ten months? Ten months earlier I was banging Luisa. It couldn't be mine, then. But maybe she froze some of my sperm. Was that even possible? But she was married, or so she said. The baby didn't look too happy about the situation. Like father, like son?

"Oh my god, he looks just like you, congratulations."

This from the waitress looking at me and then the baby as if we were biological tennis. I had been lured back to New York with the promise of a cheap East Village apartment, but now she was about to ambush me with a paternity suit. She was a lawyer; she knew all about these things. She knew I had enough money to justify the effort because she already had all my bank account details. She was laughing at me.

Thankfully Bridgit piped in with "Oh my god, no. I see what you mean, but he's just a friend."

The waitress retreated and I exhaled.

The truth was less flattering.

As an unemployed writer I fulfilled the requirement that all tenants in her building should be low-income status and preferably connected to the arts. Of the six apartments in the building, only two of the occupants met these requirements, and one of them was so old he was expected to vacate not just the apartment but his mortal frame at any moment. My addition to the roster would help reclaim some credibility for the co-op, and with my recently banked severance payment, there would be no worries about me keeping up the rent payments. In fact, if anything I was doing Bridgit a favor.

I was back in New York under my latest guise. A writer living in the East Village.

3

ELLEN

"Are you Rob?" a woman's voice said.

I looked up from my bagel and shook my head.

"No, sorry."

If she had been gorgeous I might have been less certain.

"Oh. Sorry," said the woman, smiling weakly. She sat down at the adjacent table and glared at me as if I had just lied to her. Was I, in fact, Rob?

Her face was a conspiracy of cosmetics, and I could see how her online profile might have attracted some emails, but in daylight she looked like an effigy of a young girl. The door to the café opened behind her and a bald man about my height poked his head inside. When he spotted the woman he paused, and his eyes met mine for a split second. He could have been an older version of me. He withdrew his head and disappeared. At least he wasn't fat.

My phone rang, and because I didn't recognize the number, I answered, raising a finger to the woman who sat next to me, signaling that I would be just a moment.

"Hello?"

"Hello, darling sweetie, it's Ellen."

It was the features editor of the celebrated *Prowess* magazine, and her southern accent was even more pronounced now that she was alone in her apartment. She had already described herself as "the editor of a well-known magazine" in her profile, so I knew after only a little research who she was before she called. Her voice was laced with sex from the moment I answered, and within minutes she was describing her body to me.

"I'm lying on my couch in just a T-shirt and panties."

She paused as I downloaded this mental JPEG.

"And I should warn you that my panties aren't very fashionable. They have road maps on them. I got them in Italy."

"Oh, I don't know, road maps can be useful. All roads lead to Rome, and so forth."

She giggled delightedly.

". . . and when in Rome . . ." I caught myself, realizing it was a little too public for this.

"Now stop that. I just don't want you to be disappointed when you see the real thing."

When.

As she continued to describe herself, she might have been reading a letter I'd written to a Sexual Santa.

"I have a very nice bottom. I'm always getting compliments for my bottom. My breasts aren't large, but they're well proportioned, or at least I think they are, and my nipples stick out a lot; I have to wear padded bras because they poke out through my clothing. And I have no pubic hair. None at all. I had it all lasered. I had to go back three times until . . . well . . . now it just doesn't grow back anymore."

I was silent.

If there were other sounds in the world, I was unaware of them as I got up to leave. I had to hide my semi-erection from the waiting woman, who still sat there looking at me accusingly.

I walked over the Brooklyn Bridge to meet her at Quebec Street Alehouse. She turned out to be a lot smaller and prettier than I'd expected. She still had no idea I had written a book, so for every moment I withheld this information I felt like a liar. She was literary and tasty. Nice ass too. Lovely kissable lips, and she was keen. Amazingly keen. She was all touchy, and from the moment we met, she couldn't keep her hands to herself.

"There's a book," I said.

She seemed to accept this quite quickly and nodded like it was inevitable. It was as if I had just told her I was married and she was somehow okay with it.

"Oh, there's a book, is there?"

I was about to tell her I didn't know who she worked for when we first corresponded, but I knew it would sound hollow. We walked down to the promenade and sat on a bench facing the famous Manhattan skyline. It was very romantic, but when I leaned over to kiss her, she stopped me.

"Be careful, darling, you might cut yourself."

I was sure she was referring to my twisted attempt to get published, but seeing the confusion in my eyes, she added, "On my earrings—they're very pointy."

"Fortifications against unwanted advances."

I was trying to impress her. She smiled weakly and looked across the river as if trying to decide what to do with me. We had certainly touched a lot for a first date. Up to this point she had seemed in a hurry to have me fall in love with her. I think what had impressed her most about me was the fact that I worked in advertising, and now she was beginning to realize my heart wasn't in it anymore.

Pushing out her breasts, she remarked that her shoulders were tight, and I dutifully offered to massage her compact little back. She was tight and muscular but not unpleasantly so. Her best friend was a functioning alcoholic, she said without ceremony.

"She only drinks wine . . ." and here she left a space for me to say, *Oh, well, that's okay. She's okay, then*. But I just nodded behind her now on the promenade bench.

As she continued talking, I began to feel genuinely sorry for her. Her job sounded terrible. Here she was—pretty, intelligent, literary-minded, and funny—working for a porn magazine. She took on the faraway look again when she spoke of the novel she'd written that had almost been published by Python.

"They wanted revisions and more revisions until in the end, well . . . they didn't want anything at all."

"I'd like to read it," I lied.

And then she answered an accusation I hadn't the courage to make.

"I can expose writers to much larger audiences."

She effortlessly reeled off a list of surnames and then fell conspicuously silent, the better to reap my amazement.

"That's some list," I said, only because I knew it was expected of me. I hadn't heard of even one of them.

"And Jorge Blaus has contributed more than one piece. You *have* heard of him."

"Of course I've heard of him."

"Thank God for that."

She was only half joking. How would she introduce someone so literally feral to her friends? She was so small and tightly wound that I said I'd help her uncoil, but she thought this was not the most attractive of images. I said she took my meaning to be more serpentine than spring-based. I wanted to refer to my penis in this way, but I thought it was too soon, and of course there was always the question of overclaim. For a penis to uncoil, it would need to be a lot longer than anything I could muster. Mine was more likely to de-pant than uncoil. She giggled wickedly, and as I continued to massage her crackling back, I tried to sustain an effortless demeanor in an attempt at disguising my nervousness born out of the hope that I was being interviewed for the position of Lover/Writer.

She said she had smoked some dope the previous night after her dad went back to his hotel, and I suddenly saw her more clearly for what she was. Not so much shy, as I had first thought, but angry. She apologized for her job, but she obviously enjoyed the power it gave her. Over writers, maybe? And publishers? Why not? Demanding revisions from Python would be a thrill. And I sensed she was itching to break hearts, because her apparent openness would disappear at the drop of a hat, leaving the suitor standing outside and alone. Being a writer herself, she knew that like a mother with a newborn, I'd do anything to move my precious book forward. So she can't have been in any doubt as to whether I was interested.

"You don't smoke?"

"No."

"And you don't drink?"

"No."

"Not even at Christmas?"

I shook my head.

"And you don't do drugs at all."

140

"No."

"You're like a monk."

"My middle name is Camillus. My dad actually wanted me to become a monk."

"But monks are allowed to have sex, right?"

"Of course. You read the papers—we get more sex than most."

Her tight little laugh rippled throughout her back.

"It's just as well you're impoverished, darling, because with all that charm you'd be unstoppable."

This referred to my confession that I no longer worked in advertising.

"And all the more impressive when you realize my penury is self-imposed. I'm merely being of service to humanity."

She wanted to see my bare head, so I took off my woolen skullcap and she ran her open palm over its surface.

"It's a nice shape," she said.

Maybe her dad was blue-eyed and bald too?

"It's because I'm a caesarean, no forceps: *untimely ripp'd,* dontcha know, like Macduff."

I felt fortunate to be able to harness the shape of my head to Shakespeare.

"In fact, I was as reluctant to enter Ireland as he was."

"Macduff?"

"No, Caesar."

This referred to Caesar's hesitation in conquering a

country he dubbed Hibernia (Land of Eternal Winter). If she didn't get the reference, she didn't show it.

"Send me your book," she said, stepping back and regarding me like an art exhibit. Something had happened. Something important. It had suddenly become about my book. A major decision had been made. She made me promise to "write her" when I got home safely. It was like something a mother might say. We had already hugged a few times, and it felt nice and natural. Now that we were parting, she seemed to want something more. It hadn't occurred to me to kiss her, so I hugged her again, this time for longer.

"I'm sorry. I'm being quite huggy and touchy-feely."

"It's okay. I'm not stopping you," she responded.

Not exactly gushing, but it would do.

"Never mind the book. I'm just glad you like my head."

"I'll show it to our fiction editor." And then she added with a smile, "If I like it."

This was my big chance. I was sure she'd like it. I felt like it was the most important meeting I'd ever had. An excerpt in *Prowess* would be excellent exposure.

A week later she emailed me in her official capacity as features editor of *Prowess*.

"We have a policy at *Prowess* never to print any material that is demeaning to women."

I never heard from her again.

MARIAN

I logged on to datemedotcom.

No messages.

I was sick of this. Where would it end? Even as I emptied myself into one girl I was already looking for another. A life dictated by my dick. Such behavior had made sense up to now, since I had been so nomadic, but at this point I had a rent-controlled apartment in the East Village. To a woman in New York, this was the equivalent of beer goggles. And shouldn't I at least *want* to live with a girl? Just so I could say I'd done it once? But I didn't need to try it to know that it was my idea of a nightmare. Someone peering up your ass all day. And all night.

Still, it would be nice to have someone . . . consistent. Or would it? It hadn't worked out so well with Yvette. I couldn't bear the idea of living with her. In fact, by the time we had officially broken up, I couldn't bear the sight of her. And because I'd wasted two years of her baby-making life, she hated me. But didn't I deserve another try? I looked longingly at the face of a beautiful girl staring out from a profile called sculptorgrl824445. It was time to unleash the most devious tactic of all.

Honesty.

sorry but I hate this fucking site . . . please save me from the indignity of having to sell myself in this Meat Market . . . we'll tell our friends we met in a bookshop . . . you need to

143

know that you're far too beautiful and smart to be on this thing . . . meet me in the real world and I'll read to you in my irish accent in my rent-controlled apartment and massage your feet . . . anything you say.

I hate this site too, but I like the idea of meeting in a bookshop. Her name was Marian, and after a hurried meeting in the design section of the Strand bookshop and a half-drunk cup of coffee in a nearby café, she indicated a desire to see the remastered, visually refurbished version of *Donnie Darko* that was showing the following week at the Ziegfeld Theatre. I'd get the tickets if she got the treats. Perrier and pistachios. I couldn't be sure whether she thought of me as a friend or if there really was some romantic interest there, but I liked her immediately.

It was unusually hot for October as she approached me in the crimson foyer of the cinema, so she removed her gray cardigan and stuffed it in her bag. She wore a pair of short, scuffed black boots with long black textured socks that stopped abruptly above her knees, accentuating her beautifully slender, shapely thighs as she walked. With the cardigan gone, I tried not to gape at all that clean skin racing up and down and around her arms, neck, and shoulders. The outline of her small, upturned breasts was easily discernible under the black sleeveless T-shirt.

"I neglected to get us treats," she said.

She couldn't pop into a deli and get a bag of nuts and

a bottle of seltzer on the way? I had already queued for an hour to ensure we got decent seats, and now I was being told I was to go treatless for three hours in a pair of jeans that were too tight for me. I must have made some sort of face, because after disappearing for a while she returned with *one* bag of popcorn and *one* bottle of Perrier and handed them both to me. Now I had treats, but she had nothing. I felt like a selfish complaining bastard. But this was the moment she first exposed me to one of her smiles, which seemed to gather every molecule of my being around it like hobos to a handout. Even the people in the line seemed to shuffle closer.

Now I felt like a *lucky* selfish complaining bastard.

She seemed to like me, but I couldn't be sure it was romantic. It had to be. Otherwise, wouldn't she have to say something? But being newly arrived from Iowa, she might not know the rules of engagement. Would I be referred to as a friend in her next carefully worded email?

It became important to understand what I was dealing with. If she was just looking for a friend, I would need to be careful, because this girl was far too easy to fall in love with. After the film ended, we both took the subway together downtown. During the trip I was treated to retina-scorching glimpses of her clean-skinned thighs as she rearranged herself in the subway seat beside me according to the shift and shove of the carriage. It was like a dance. Did she know I was enjoying this so much? I had an urge to lift her straight up out of her seat and position her on my lap.

The train's vibration would do the rest.

I shouldn't have been able get away with ogling her so much, but she didn't seem to take any notice of me. She didn't even look at me when she spoke, which wasn't often. It was as if she welcomed my scrutiny, but it made me feel like a pervert. She didn't ask one question about me all night. Not one. I even checked my reflection in the subway window to make sure I was visible. This beautiful uninterested girl unnerved me. And I wasn't alone. Other guys on the subway looked at her too. Long, lingering, wistful looks. They wasted no time looking jealously at me.

I watched her reflection to see if she checked herself out in the subway windows. To see if she herself gained any satisfaction from her power. I wanted to dismiss her as conceited. But she seemed not to notice. She didn't check herself out even once. It simply wasn't her fault she was beautiful. In fact, if anything, she was careful where she looked. Maybe she was so accustomed to being looked at that she had learned to lower her eyes. It certainly didn't appear to be something she enjoyed. Men's lust and women's jealousy.

I, on the other hand, looked like an idiot that night because I hadn't worn my favorite jeans. I had washed them specially, but they hadn't been dry in time. And why had it been so hot in October? I began to sweat when we had to scramble around in the subway station looking for the 6 train platform in the airlessness. At one point I saw her incredulous look as those cool blue-gray eyes registered the dark sweat stains seeping through my shirt like bullet wounds.

She was beautiful, calm, and aloof. I was sweating.

And as if to confirm this, I heard nothing more from her after we said good-bye that first night. Was that it? It was so rude. It was as if she had decided not to bother with me.

It seemed so wasteful. So punk rock. So Goth.

Had it been my choice of clothing?

For seven days and seven nights I ignored all sorts of primal and spiritual urges to contact her. If she had told me to fuck off and die, I would have welcomed the clarity with hysterical laughter, but to hear nothing at all was torture.

> *Your method of letting me know you're not interested (i.e., totally ignoring me) is uncalled for. If, after reading the online excerpt from my book, you got frightened, I guess I have to accept that, but it's a novel, after all . . . Would you be afraid to meet the writer of a murder mystery? If you're not interested, period, then of course that's fine too, but don't you think one short email is in order? You seemed quite down-to-earth to me, and I'm amazed at myself to be writing this email, but I couldn't have you think I was okay with just being ignored . . . Anyway, good luck.*

My screen shuddered as I clicked send, and as it re-adjusted, there was an email from her. I thought it was one of those "I'm out of the office" replies, but no, it was her response to the email I'd sent the previous week thanking her for a nice evening at the movies.

> *it's raining outside . . . i'm working away making belt buckles, sawing and filing, this will be my weekend, i think it's likely that i will be sitting at this same spot solidly for the next 3 days. but i will definitely let you know if there's a break in the clouds. literally as well as figuratively, it seems, and maybe we can hang out again:)*

Her friendly email arrived just as my pissy, self-centered, bile-filled epistle went out. Had I received it ten seconds earlier, she would never have known my feelings of hurt at the absence of her communication. Encouraged that she was at least open to hanging out again, I asked if she'd like to visit the Met during the week, and her response was so half-hearted I suggested we do it some other time. She sounded relieved. It was as if I had freed her from a disgusting obligation.

"Thank you for being so understanding."

It stung that she should thank me for the opportunity *not* to meet me. But such rebuttals made me want her even more. My biggest fear was that she saw me as a friend. That I was entering the Eunuchery. That I would fall totally in love with her while she sat there innocent of all charges.

Her smile tranquilized me.

What did it matter if I was only her friend? It was nice being with her, wasn't it? We had a nice time together, didn't we? I was enjoying myself, wasn't I? My logic would rear up against the anesthetic only to succumb to a pleasant complacency and peace. Why did I need to fuck her? Why did I need to fuck all women everywhere except my mother? What was wrong with me? The act of having sex with her would protect me from being emotionally bruised. If I could persuade her (and myself) that I was only after sex, then my emotional involvement had to have been an act. She'd have been duped by the master forger. And there she was, thinking I was in love with her. How naive the poor girl would seem. The sex would be my deposit. My safety net.

My safety pin.

And then, during an impromptu meeting in a coffee shop initiated by a text from her saying she'd unexpectedly found a parking space near my apartment, she let her hair down for the first time, and that was that.

My god, she was beautiful.

She looked so relaxed and refreshed I had to actively wrench my eyes away to prevent intoxication. I could only afford to take little sips in the form of micro-glances. She blushed noticeably and tilted her head in a way that gave me the impression she felt something too. Either that or she saw I was smitten and sympathized.

Yea, bewareth, step ye not so gleefully into the abyss.

I'd had plenty of time to prepare my defenses against the paralyzing effects of that devastating smile and the hypnotism conjured by those dizzyingly blue-gray eyes—so soothing and exciting at the same time—but now that they were flanked by curtains of dark, shiny hair, something inside me quaked. I was reminded of my first real encounter with female beauty; in my mother's knitting catalogues I found pictures of beautiful pale Irish girls modeling cardigans. Marian had the kind of face I could stare at for hours, and I used every conversational trick I had to do exactly that. She seemed aware of her beauty but determined to hide it. Or hide from it.

From time to time she'd twist her face into an ugly expression to save me from the full brunt of her seduction. As if embarrassed by her wealth, she needed to play it down. And the more self-effacing she appeared, the more perplexed I became.

Was she interested in me only because I had mentioned there was another rent-controlled apartment vacant in my building? Would she suffer untold indignities to get into it? Was she merely waiting to confirm that I had money stashed in London and Amsterdam? After three hours of walking around downtown Manhattan with her, there was still nothing I could confidently point at that indicated I should make a move on her. Meanwhile, her body language mumbled all manner of half-heard obscenities.

She pushed out those lovely pert breasts and twirled a finger in her lovely heavy, dark hair. She held my gaze in hers and refreshed her lip gloss not just once but twice. When we stopped for a coffee, she drew my attention to her boots, turning them sideways to point at the fraying of the soles caused by our long walks, and in doing so, she crossed and recrossed those clean, lean legs, showing me far more than was necessary. Was she just teasing me? Was this something she got off on? Or was she unaccustomed to giving the come-on and I was simply missing it?

I could plainly see other guys out of the range of her peripheral vision enjoying the sensation of looking at her unhindered by any need to be polite. I looked for opportunities to move things forward. I was still wary of being cast as the friend of this beautiful, scruffy girl. When she made even the slightest effort, she was stunning. And that smile was celestial.

Celestial.

I felt sorry for her having to be seen with me. It was obvious she could do so much better. Maybe it was because she had recently broken up with a guy she described as "very pretty" and "very tall" and "very rich." Surely I was just a consoling gnome trotting along beside her, yelping happily every time she flashed a smile. I didn't feel worthy of playing the male lead, but I wasn't about to cheat myself out of the chance of getting close to that body either. If any sexual crumbs fell off the table, I'd be there. She was definitely worth the wait, if waiting was what I was doing.

At worst I would learn how to behave around beauty and could use my findings on future prospects. And in the meantime I could at least pretend I was with her.

She liked to walk around downtown visiting historic sites, and I was quite happy with this idea, because walking was perfect for making a move. And inexpensive.

And there was something nice about just getting to know her as a friend. Most of her friends were guys, she said. This was an ominous sign. It meant women couldn't stand being around her because she was naturally slim and beautiful, and men would do anything to get into her pants, including pretend to be her friend.

The last thing she said before disappearing into the subway on New Year's was "I have to start looking for an apartment in Manhattan."

It was as if she wanted me to be clearly briefed for the year ahead. Did she want me only for my two-bedroom apartment? She was sharing with a roommate she didn't get along with. Was I merely real estate to her?

This had to stop.

We went walking again a week later. She looked great in a pair of tight blue jeans spattered with white paint. She had a tight little ass in there. God help me. She was so feisty and sprightly that I thought I had better make a move soon or she wouldn't be single for much longer. Some guy would approach her on a subway or in a café or in the street, and that'd be the end of me. We sat on a bench in Union Square, and as we chatted and laughed at the squirrels, she played with her hair and shoved out those breasts and even touched my knee not just once but twice.

"I'd really like to kiss you," I said.

The squirrels froze in mid-nibble as an excruciating silence descended. It was so prolonged that it seemed intentionally cruel. I should apologize. Make a joke. I had ruined everything. Feet together, she inspected her boots. I risked a look, and instead of the beautiful smile, there was only a lipless line.

"I'm not ready," she said, more to herself than anyone else. And suddenly she just appeared extraordinarily vain. After all, it's no fun being out of reach if no one's reaching. And I was reaching. I had been reluctant to bring up the kiss at all, but I was torn between a fear that she might be insulted if I didn't, since we'd been seeing each other so often, and a gung ho need to at least get the subject aired.

"Okay," I said, "but I just wanted you to know that I'd like to."

There was a second uncomfortable pause, and though I sensed my plea was being considered, I'd had enough for one night. I had a sudden need to do some rejecting of my own. "Okay, let's get you to a subway."

After a joyless hug at the subway station, where nothing more than our jackets touched, I walked home feeling bruised and used but glad I had tried. I hoped I'd never see her again. I would concentrate on my book.

Maybe I'd use the AA meetings to find literary contacts.

There were so many well-connected people attending meetings all over the city that it seemed wasteful not to approach one of them. I would routinely sit beside Cute-E, Simon Reeves, Pat Nillon, Anthony Sherts, Ulrich Wapton—writers, actors, models, and millionaires. People less principled than I turned up at meetings *pretending* to be alcoholics just to network.

When I lived in London, years before, I myself had sponsored a young actor who has since become a household name. Even as I write this he is still one of the most sought-after male leads for action movies in the country. But it was obvious back then that in asking me to sponsor him he was hoping to get a part in a commercial. And I, hoping to trick him into getting sober, encouraged him to believe he might succeed. But he was too clever for me. He had already taken the precaution of asking two other well-placed AA members to sponsor him so that he could decide which of us would provide the best opportunity. He stopped calling after only a few days, and I assumed he'd gone back to drinking. But then a few months later, on a director's showreel, I was faced with one of the most sobering images I'd ever seen.

He had landed a part in a whiskey commercial.

The concept involved twins (both played by my ex-sponsee) philosophizing about the nature of dark and light while perhaps inwardly deciding whether to trade his sobriety for an acting career. The historic moment where he quaffs thirstily from the abyss is preserved forever. Lots of AA members relapse and drink again. But not many have had their slips televised. Nowadays he is often featured in the media, throwing wild punches at photographers outside nightclubs. There's an ad for AA in there somewhere.

Can you forgive me for being such a teenager the other night? Although her text, a week after the Union Square incident, acknowledged my disappointment, it still didn't offer anything even resembling hope. She had driven in from Williamsburg in her champagne-colored Olaffson, and if I wanted to go for a drive, *she'd be game*. This expression had vaguely sexual connotations for me, but I knew it wasn't how she meant it. And although I would have loved to take her up on the offer, she had to be punished for refusing my advances. I felt I had to protect myself from getting any more involved with her.

Her offer of a drive felt like a platonic consolation for a sexually rejected buddy. I replied simply with a link to my advertising website in the hopes that it would show her I wasn't just some penniless idiot who should count himself lucky to be with her and that, if anything, it was the other way around. I hadn't really gone into detail about my advertising work because I wanted her to think of me as a bohemian writer. My intention now was to show her how accomplished I was, while at the same time denying her access. I didn't think I'd ever be able to be so proud of my advertising work, especially in art circles, but it was beginning to look like I could.

An hour later, which in my mind was enough time to check out my website and understand just how award-winning and internationally fucking wonderful I was, she texted me again: *the girl just wasn't ready . . . try again you will have more success.* Wearying though it was to be proven right, I wasn't going to refuse.

After a faultless dinner at a medium-priced Tibetan restaurant where we split the bill, I invited her back to my fur-lined lair. She looked lovely. There was something almost Midwestern about her manner, as if she had yet to be Manhattanized. Her hair looked like Princess Leia crossed with Pippi Longstocking, and I liked it because she had obviously spent time on it. It was now just a question of where and when we would kiss.

There was a certain sadness attached to this realization. I was unkissable as a lowly writer, but for an award-winning advertising man she spent two hours on her hair? My nagging doubt persisted even as I nudged her gently against the railings of Tompkins Square Park, kissing for the first time in the cool January air.

She flicked her tongue gently across mine, and for a moment I wanted to just jam her against the railings, but it felt too disrespectful. Instead we strolled back to my place, pretending to be interested in what we saw on the way. I fumbled my keys at both doors, and since I'd made such a big deal out of having bought Barry's Tea from Cork, she stood dutifully still while I went through the motions of putting on the kettle.

When I turned around, it was into a deep, longing, yearning kiss. I felt her reach behind me to turn off the stove. She pulled back and looked at me now with the hope-filled eyes of a lover. No more ambiguity. Why? Because I had money? Because the apartment was nicer than she'd expected? Why did it even matter?

If only she had kissed me the first time in Union Square.

I stepped forward and she stepped back, and we waltzed like that, kissing to the bedroom. On the bed we shoved ourselves together, and unbuttoning her jeans, I ventured a fingertip toward the prize. I refrained, though, from slipping a finger inside her, partly out of respect and partly from fear of rejection. Instead I very gently skimmed those pursed lips for what seemed like an inordinate length of time. The silence became tangible, as if our futures depended on the next infinitesimal motion of my index finger.

I could feel moisture seeping out of the beautifully trimmed seam. Had she known she would let me proceed this far? Was I just catching up with what she had already decided? Either way, the moment of immersion was audibly welcomed.

I can't say for sure, but I think she might have come right there on my fingers. I say this because as I continued to touch her very gently, she shivered involuntarily and moaned deeply like she was on very strong drugs. I was pleased with this, of course, and congratulated myself on having thawed her out at last.

After a moment she arranged herself on top of me and lay there kissing and breathing warmly on my neck and ear. Her jeans were opened even more now, and her groin was positioned directly over the hot bulge in my jeans.

"Let me introduce you to somebody," I whispered, trying to be casual, but I was already drunk with lust. Deftly opening the top two buttons of my jeans, she exposed the tip of my cock and began flicking her fingers across it so maddeningly that I almost came immediately.

I had to stop her because I wasn't ready for such an upheaval. It seemed too barbaric compared with the gentle, unrushed atmosphere that had led us to this point. But I didn't want her to think her skill was unappreciated.

I was amazed at her skill. Amazed, thrilled, and worried.

If she was this good and this beautiful, then I was in danger of . . . well, yes, of falling in love. But there was hope. The one area where she was still untested. If her ass proved to be a misshapen mess that looked good only when locked in by tight jeans, then I could let myself off the hook and breathe a sigh of relief. I let my hand stray downward.

"Oh, fuck."

She laughed, but I couldn't have been more serious. Her ass was superb. All my criteria had been met, and somehow it was devastating. I was a castaway inconvenienced by rescue.

• • • •

In the foyer of the Metropolitan Museum of Art, Marian approached me in scuffed boots, woolen tights, a leather miniskirt, and an open coat. She looked like one of those girls on her way to a date with some lucky bastard other than me. That she looked great was in itself something to celebrate, but the realization that she had dressed like this specifically for me elevated my senses to such a degree that I gushed with gratitude.

We sauntered between the Greek and Roman statues, which merely confirmed for me how well proportioned and beautifully made she was. I pointed my phone at the statues, but the pictures I took were of her. Smiling. Standing. Walking. Pouting.

"It's because you're so well made, that's why you have such a feel for three-dimensional objects. You instinctively know when something is beautiful because it meets the standards of craftsmanship that you yourself represent."

Yes, I actually said that to her.

She beamed at this and stepped effortlessly into a rockstar pose, one hand on her hip and head tilted in mock defiance. I took the first picture that so many men would later drool over, and at that moment I realized I was in love with her. It had been creeping upon me like the flu, but now it was full-blown.

Almost as suddenly the evening began to disintegrate.

We couldn't find a place to eat. The Venezuelan place that I had bragged about being near my street in the East Village was overrun with little nasal gnomes from New Jersey, and the lovely Marian was actually beginning to show signs of being seriously dissatisfied. Pissed, even. Couldn't she at least pretend to be polite? Had I blown it? Maybe this was what she was really like, and the rest had been an act. As a last resort we ducked into Le Couloir, which was pricey but worth it in the end, because after a burger (the cheapest thing we could find on the menu), she was fine again.

"What would you like to do now?" I said, fully prepared to walk her to the subway.

"Let's have some more of that tea we never end up drinking."

There was only one response to that.

Lying there afterward, I felt as if a huge magnet had been lowered over me and all the sharp metal filings and ground-down iron fragments that had been circulating in my body and mind had been magically lifted out of me and replaced with warm honey.

"You come like a woman," she said.

And there it was: Marian's famous smile.

Hoping to capture it, I reached for my phone, but somehow I got her midriff instead. This was the second picture. Lying facedown in a pair of tight white panties and dark gray woolen thigh-high tights on my nice clean duvet that I had spent three days washing and drying, she looked like an ad for underwear. She blushed at the sight of my cock hardening again. And after having just come, she was so erotic and wholesome and dark at the same time that it seemed like a duty to be erect. It was a salute. This was when I took the third picture.

Transfixed, I stared at her image on my phone.

Later I was looking for something on the Internet when she crept up from behind and perched on the backrest of my chair, which effectively leveled her pussy with the back of my neck. I felt its hot breath against my skin. I picked her up, trekked back into the bedroom, and sat us both down on the bed. We began the sort of feverish kissing that could culminate only in orgasm.

The fact that I was showing no interest at all in other girls had itself become worrisome. My profile was still active, but my heart just wasn't in it. The more I thought about it, the more I found myself in unprecedented territory: if I already had a fantastic girl, why would I need to keep looking for more? But I had always thought I'd end up with a French girl. In France. Paris, the city of love, and all that. But Marian looked more French than Yvette. If I had been casting a photo shoot of my ideal woman, Marian would have probably gotten the job.

But there was still *the phone thing*.

This was our shorthand for the fact that I could never seem to talk to her on the phone. I'd feel anger rise inside me like a tide and have to resist throwing the phone at the wall. I tried to explain that I had trouble speaking into the gappy cell phone service and that I preferred to speak to her in person. This was partly true, but the real reason was simple but unutterable. When she was physically present, the combination of her scent, beauty, and fashion sense seemed to gently cup my libido. Those impossibly slender thighs extending from the ever-present knee socks countered any upsets caused by such Americanisms as *hey you* or *goofball*. But on the phone she had no such ambassadors. Her dismembered voice offered no protection from the fact that I was, for the first time in my life, not just in love, but in love with an American.

How could I have let this happen?

And it was almost impossible to bring her to orgasm. She'd repeatedly reposition my fingers over an area that seemed so far north of where I would normally have set up camp that I thought she was joking. On more than one occasion she removed my hand altogether, not so much in disgust as in resignation. Didn't she realize she was discarding a technique that had worked for a large number of satisfied women? Apparently the very pretty, very rich, very tall guy she dated before me had actually gotten angry with her because she took so long to come.

I feigned surprise. "Angry? Really? Why?"

"Yeah, right? I mean, after all, it's my body."

Secretly I knew exactly what he meant.

How insultingly boring it was to be down there lapping away on god knows what for god knows how long, with each moan from the head office just another false promise of promotion. And when, after what felt like hours, she did erupt, her orgasm was dwarfed by my sense of relief. But even as I made them, I knew such protestations were merely last-ditch attempts at denial. I was in love.

New York was full of women who wanted to be with the writer of "a surprise dark-horse Williamsburg bestseller." It wasn't as if I couldn't get another girl. And yet Marian was so darkly sexual. One of the things I liked about her being a drama magnet was that she enjoyed being spanked for her transgressions. When she lost her apartment keys, we were locked out for three hours in the freezing cold until an upstairs neighbor happened along and let us in. I spent those hours thinking up spank-ideas. I settled on one where I cut a stencil of my name out of thin cardboard and spanked it onto her lovely pale buttocks. I'm happy to be able to say that this is exactly what I did.

As she walked ahead of me up the steps to her apartment I was drawn forward in a sort of hypnotic trance, meekly following that ass. Tabernacle and supplicant.

She looked over her shoulder knowingly, and I knew that she knew she had me, and I didn't care. So what if she was only after an apartment or my paltry savings—I didn't care. Everything that had taken place in my life up to that point had occurred only so that I could truthfully say I was a writer living in New York with a beautiful girlfriend with a beautiful ass that had my name scorched onto it.

The familiar hints began to be dropped.

How draining it was to have to continuously talk her off the ledge. If only her roommate wasn't always so depressed. The rent was cheap and they were old friends, but she felt like an unpaid live-in therapist. She'd stop talking abruptly. This was my cue to suggest we move in together.

Which I ignored.

And when she began smiling at babies and old couples, I suppose I could have at least feigned interest in starting some sort of family, but I just didn't. Or couldn't. And I see now that my continued presence online was my attempt at arranging a fallback relationship in case Marian left me. Insurance against getting hurt. Or maybe I was just addicted to being online. One night after checking my messages on her computer, I forgot to sign out.

LAURA

Laura, there you are, unsocked and de-panted and all alone on a saturday night . . . I'm thinking of you lying on your bed touching yourself slowly, gently. In my fantasy your hands would suddenly become my hands . . . it might be fun to discuss this further over the phone . . . are evenings good for you?

The fact that Marian stumbled upon this message was particularly galling because, in the year and a half we'd been together, I had never invited her on a phone date like that. Not to mention our issues with *the phone thing*. But the telesexual invite was nothing compared to the spiritual infidelity.

I have since asked myself a thousand times how I could have let it happen. Maybe on some level I wanted her to read it. She was getting too close to the inner sanctum. She was almost in. With my defenses reduced to rubble around me, I felt it was time to surrender or self-destruct. Or maybe I yearned for the familiarity of unhappiness, choosing self-sabotage over uncertainty. I'd rather fuck it up than not know. When I look back, it's obvious that we were finished the moment she read that email, but it took a year to sink in. To all appearances we were still together, and she'd laugh and smile and even agree to help me reach orgasm from time to time, but she wasn't necessarily in the room when she did it. She made a point of staying clothed, and if I tried to unbutton anything, her free hand would come up involuntarily and push mine away.

A hand job is a great way to keep a guy at arm's length.

I tried to explain that I hadn't been looking for girls so much as customers for my book. She thought about this for a moment. She was trying to be fair. Why not give me the benefit of the doubt? I wasn't all that bad. I had some good points. And yet how could I? Didn't I realize how much I'd hurt her? She was forcing herself to try on my ill-fitting skin, to look at the world through my eyes.

"If that's true, then why don't you let me help sell your book?"

Was she trying to smoke me out? Call my bluff? If I really was just selling books, then I wouldn't need to hide the fact from her. Surely I'd be happy to have her help me.

I could even show her the messages and ask her opinion about how to improve my pitch. But, sadly, this was not an option. I had been actively pursuing all manner of female, since the very first day Marian and I had met. In fact, the only reason we'd been together for so long was because I'd had this emotional escape route. This vent. Whenever Marian canceled on me, which was often, I was able to receive the news calmly and lovingly. She didn't need to know I was seriously pissed because I'd be denied sex that night or that I avenged myself by sending out ten or fifteen messages to new online prospects. And yes, it was true that I mentioned the book and the fact that it was available in bookstores, but only because it might help get me laid. Was there some way I could incorporate Marian in the sale of books? Not with girls; that just wasn't going to work. But when I imagined a guy clicking on my new photos of Marian in a datemedot com profile, I blushed with emotion. It was too fucked-up to be love. But it was close.

FRANCOISE

Likes literature, cinema, and sex . . . maybe even all at the same time.

This was the headline for a new datemedotcom profile featuring some of the sexier pictures I'd taken of Marian. Her face was either cropped out or in shadow so that there was no chance of her being recognized. I was careful to ensure that there were no reflections on surfaces where her face might show. There were one or two pictures I'd taken of her standing in front of a glass doorway in the West Village where she was gently backlit, and in her boots and shorts she looked gorgeous. I muffled twinges of guilt under thin layers of justification. This whole thing had been her idea. She had initiated it. I told myself she'd be flattered I was incorporating her into my life. My art. I'd launch the profile just to see

167

if it worked. If it didn't, there would be no need to mention it to her, and if it did, then I could present it as a successful project based completely around her, which, if I was clever, could be perceived as a testament to her beauty.

Meanwhile I trembled with glee because I knew I'd stumbled on the perfect marketing tool. I lost myself in the writing and design of a project worthy of my talents. In the end I flattered myself that the four shots I selected for this new, totally fictitious but seemingly authentic profile were of a sufficiently high standard that the photographer who took them could be considered at least semiprofessional.

Username
Beautifullylit

Age
23

Body type
Thin/petite (I get most of my clothes from the children's section at Old Navy.)

Languages
French/English/Italian

Occupation
Photographer/Assistant/Model/Writer

Last great book I read
Diary of an Oxygen Thief *by Anonymous. It's a little scary but brilliant too. I highly recommend it.*

Superpower you would most like to possess
To read minds

Most humbling moment
I'll tell you later . . . it involves farm machinery.

Celebrity I most resemble
After being told I look like Jane Birkin so many times I looked her up, and it turns out we have the same measurements, so maybe there's something to it!

More about me
Okay, the farm machinery thing. I realize it might be misleading, so I want to make it clear. I wasn't disfigured in any way . . . my summer dress was sucked right off me by a potato grader . . . not as humbling in France as it would have been here (the workers hardly even noticed), but embarrassing all the same.

Favorite onscreen sex scene
The best sex takes place on the cutting-room floor.

No messages. A twenty-three-year-old purportedly French photographer/writer with a gorgeous ass didn't get even one reply? Maybe it was because her face was hidden. Maybe they thought she was disfigured. Even after adding the disclaimer about the farm machinery, she was still getting no responses.

If, as I told Marian, I had been on datemedotcom only to sell books, I was now feeling the pressure to prove it. I had told her I was trying something out, and reporting back to her with a result of zero messages and therefore zero sales seemed somehow to indicate that I had been lying about my earlier claims.

Hotlisting was a way of indicating interest without actually sending a message. If you were hotlisted, a little flame graphic appeared on your profile with the name of the person who thought you were hot. As in the real world, men were expected to make the first move, but hotlisting was an acceptable method for a lady to indicate interest.

I hotlisted every male I could find in the New York area. Old, young, handsome, ugly—every guy I could find, and even some girls who indicated interest in women.

It was one sure way to make sure they got an eyeful of Francoise's ass when they clicked on the profile to see who had hotlisted them. Everyone was eligible, from the hipsters with clever headlines (this is your caption speaking) to the old men who barely bothered to fill out the questions because they knew they'd never get a response anyway (just looking). By the time I was finished, they were all aflame.

But when I logged on, there were still no messages.

Really?

If I had been hotlisted by a beautiful girl with the body of a supermodel in varying degrees of undress, I'd feel duty-bound to at least reply in case there was an outside chance of my fucking her. It didn't make sense. I studied the profiles more carefully.

Maybe I hadn't been attentive enough. I'd send each individual a specific message relating to the rubbish mentioned in their profile. To make each message personal would mean a lot more work, though the extra burden was negligible if my efforts translated to sales. I began tailoring emails to specific profiles: *If you liked* Trainspotting, *you'll love* Diary of an Oxygen Thief. I was about to send this message to a mousy-looking guy who most certainly didn't look like he was accustomed to being approached by beautiful girls when I noticed that under the option *Send him an email* there was a little subheading that read *He sent you an email 3 days ago.* This was maddening, of course, because when I clicked on Beautifullylit's inbox, it showed *0 messages.* Maybe he had included his phone number and contact details and had therefore been disqualified. The site didn't like people exchanging such information because, naturally, this would put them out of business. Or maybe it just took a few days for messages to show up.

Then I noticed that below the inbox there was a little section entitled *Preferences.* I clicked on it, and there, slithering over one another like newly netted fish, were hundreds upon hundreds of glistening messages.

Seven hundred sixty-three, to be exact. I now saw that the default setting in the Preferences section was calibrated to allow only ideal matches through to the inbox. I was looking for responses from anyone from any area as long as they were capable of buying a book. I hadn't filled out the Preferences section because I had no preferences. It was the digital equivalent of striking oil.

There were so many messages that I couldn't quite grasp the significance of what was happening. My glee peaked and dissolved into fear. Would I be the perpetrator of my own undoing? Would this be how I lost her? I'd be instrumental in her meeting some very pretty, very rich, very tall guy from datemedotcom. But it was flattering that all these men wanted my girlfriend. Her popularity was making me more possessive of her. And I was struck by how polite their advances were. I felt like I was being given an insight into what it was like to be a beautiful girl in a world of salivating men. It was hugely flattering and terribly frightening at the same time. I suddenly saw Marian's position. Why she sometimes tried to make herself uglier. It was degrading to be admired purely because of the physical shape of your face, body, hips, and tits. But such considerations quickly evaporated when I thought of both her perfect ass and all the books I could sell. Twisted, yes. But it's the truth.

I was now living in New York without a job. My severance wasn't going to last forever. I would need to make money somehow, and it wasn't as if I was leveraging this profile and her body without her knowledge. It had been her idea. If I had been in love with her before, now I was in awe.

And I was getting a glimpse of what life was like for her and for women in general. Having so many men, from such diverse backgrounds—uncouth, urbane, entrepreneurial, blue collar, white collar—standing patiently in line to get to her put her beauty into concrete perspective. I decided not to tell her exactly how many messages she had received. I couldn't risk the possibility that she might put a stop to it. Not yet. Even seventy was a potentially scary number of men to have peering into your existence.

I told her seventeen people responded.

This was flattering without being overwhelming—though nothing, of course, compared to the reality of Francoise's inbox. Would she be curious to see if there was someone she liked?

I know I would. But then the profile represented a twenty-three-year-old French photographer/writer, not a thirty-six-year-old would-be sculptor from Poland Springs. Mind you, most guys probably wouldn't give a shit once they actually met her, but it would definitely be a hurdle. And the more hurdles I could arrange around her, the more fenced in she'd be, and the safer I'd feel.

The book was already mentioned under *Last great book I read*, but nobody was going to actually buy it just because it was mentioned. They needed some incentive. They'd buy a book only if they thought there was a chance of getting laid. I tried to remember what had piqued my interest. It was the fleeting presence that fascinated me most. The hot and cold ambiguity of the replies. The girls who would arrange to meet and then cancel on the day—*I'm sooo sorry*—and then take the sting out of it by adding the word *baby*. The way they'd casually announce a willingness to fuck, but only on the condition that I didn't fall in love. Could I pull this off? I strove to emulate just such a delicate balance with my first customer, whose headline announced a fondness for the work of the French writer Balzac. *I have a friend who refers to him as* Ballsack. *If you like his writing, you might like* Diary of an Oxygen Thief.

Ballsack? Was I out of my fucking mind? A French girl would never say that. I fretted over my technique. Surely I had been too obvious. I had read that when Stanley Kubrick created a new character, he would invent childhood memories for them: the school they attended, their first kiss, where they holidayed, their parents' relationship, a knee injury. Maybe I should have waited until at least the third email before blurting out the title of the book. *hahahaha ballsack??? that's hilarious . . . I haven't heard of that book but it sounds interesting . . . I'll check it out.*

He was thrilled to receive any sort of reply from a beautiful twenty-three-year-old French girl. It was becoming clear that another foolproof method for creating convincingly lifelike characters was to ensure they had a world-class ass. A great ass could bend reality. After a few more attempts I settled on an approach that presented the book as a personality test, the reward for which would be access to Francoise. *have you read* Diary of an Oxygen Thief? *I find I can tell a lot about a guy from his reaction to it. Are you game?*

One guy asked me to elaborate on the farm machinery thing: *you were in france? is that your home? j'adore la france.* The fact that he had ignored the salacious image I had inserted in his head just confirmed how dishonest these exchanges were. Any normal guy would be forgiven for at least referring to the idea of a semi-naked girl in a field full of French workers. The omission was so conspicuous that it was like complimenting a stripper on her nail varnish. *I'll pick up a copy of oxygen thief on my way home.*

My toes were awiggle.

The older guys were so thrilled they didn't care if it was real or not. *You're young enough to be my daughter, but I'm okay with that.*

If a beautiful, sexy girl recommended a book because it was a good barometer of character, I'd assume she was just protecting her interests. Online dating was a treacherous, conniving world where men would do anything to get into the pants of a girl like this. Francoise was merely filtering out the bad ones, the bad eggs—at least, that's how I hoped it appeared. It was a simple test to see if they were worth meeting. One thing was sure; they would never suspect she was a guy posing as a fictional character suggesting they read a true story purporting to be a novel.

I was getting a glimpse of what it was like to be intelligent and female in a world of drooling men. Guys who had ticked *financial* or *medical* to indicate their profession felt comfortable offering tips on how to improve my photography. Why did they assume they knew better than a student of photography? Because they were men, and I was just some little bitch. That's why. One idiot suggested I *boost the levels*, as if the shot was mistakenly shadowy. Then another guy pretended he'd read the book when it was obvious he'd only read an online review. When he offered to pose for me, I asked him to send some pictures, and he sent three pictures of himself naked, with a huge, frightening pole of flesh sticking out of his midsection. *what do you need me for? you could fuck yourself with that*, I demurred before blocking him. It was fun being female and beautiful. To actually *be* the object of desire. A living, breathing potential possession. But in reality, the possession, by sheer force of its magnetism, was the real owner.

One young guy volunteered to fly me to Mexico to see the Mayan villages while we got high on shrooms. Another guy, older but well maintained, offered a private box at the opera and dinner at Le Cirque; yet another, a businessman with not a suit in sight, wanted to know my preference in hotels and my shoe size, so he could lay out some options for when I arrived. Young couples invited me for drinks *no strings attached*. Out-of-town husbands were careful to mention their expense accounts. Filmmakers gave me two thumbs up. Architects asked me about my plans. Journalists promised to report back. Chefs said I sizzled.

Applicants all.

It was tempting to fuck with them.

Oh, how I could have fucked with them. I wasn't even sure how much of this was legal. I didn't want to get into any real trouble. Mischief was one thing, but crime was another. It was as if I'd broken through into some forbidden, never-before-seen realm like a pharaoh's tomb. I felt a strange sense of responsibility. Mustn't knock anything over. Just take what you need. No more. Somehow I reasoned that if I just confined myself to selling books, I wouldn't be accused of desecration and would therefore be spared the wrath of the curse. It would be regarded as artistic experimentation. A happening. As soon as they acquired the book, I was finished with them.

On the other end of the scale, there were the less confident respondents. These were guys who knew they didn't have a chance but felt they better send something because *hey, you never know, she might have a thing for short, fat, bald, older guys.* I had the power to lift these unsunned, gnarly gnomes aloft.

To absolve them.

And, grateful to find themselves within spurting distance of my mighty vagina, they wobbled away to buy my book. But it couldn't last. I would have to tell Marian before it went too far, and when that happened, I knew she'd want me to stop, which I really didn't want to do. What I wanted to do was select each state and systematically hotlist every guy I could find and recommend the book ceaselessly until I'd exhausted every city and backwoods town this wonderful country had to offer. After all, Barnes & Noble had stores in every major city in the United States, and I had access to datemedotcom's members in all of them.

I didn't overtly need to say Francoise was French in her profile; I merely included *French* in her *Languages spoken* section. And because she was female, there was no need to send out initial messages, since the men were expected to make the first move. Each email was subtle and polite on the surface, but trace it back to its source, and there was a stiffening dick. It was fascinating to watch these guys wrestle with the same subject I myself had spent so many hours trying to perfect. They approached gently, as if nearing a skittish lamb, and even though my headline was fairly bold—*Likes literature, cinema, and sex . . . maybe even all at the same time*—very few made any actual reference to it. In my thigh-high stockings, showing my ass to total strangers, I was hardly demure, but these mealymouthed modern males had been so consistently conditioned to conceal their true desires under courteous cloaks they made a girl feel dirty standing there in her underwear. In response to my beautiful, jaw-dropping ass, all they could say was *I find you intriguing*? No mention of what they'd like to do to me? The lines between fantasy and reality started to blur. A soon as I logged on to datemedotcom, I became Francoise, and she became me. After one guy went on and on about some excruciating pseudo-intellectual treatise on photography, he broke down and got to the point: *by the way, do you like to be tied up?*

By the way? Surely this was what he wanted to know in the first place. I responded: *No, not really. Do you like to be gagged? Because you sure talk a lot before getting to the point.* Delete. Block.

The guy behind the counter at St. Mark's Bookshop was pleasantly suspicious.

"I know you're doing something, I just don't know what."

"It's crazy, isn't it?" I said innocently.

"Well, whatever it is, we're burning through the copies."

If he inquired where these eager customers heard about this little literary oddity, they were not going to say "A hot French girl with a gorgeous ass from an online dating site wanted me to read it as a prerequisite to fucking her."

No.

They were going to say a friend recommended it. This would translate to the booksellers as that most coveted of sales phenomena. Word of Mouth.

It was becoming obvious that men would do or say anything to get into the pants of a twenty-three-year-old French girl, and it didn't stop at age fifty or even sixty. There were no exceptions, only variations. One guy, a Brit, tried to play on my insecurity when he accused me of *oozing entitlement.* He had correctly guessed that among the fawning emails such an approach would stand out. It was interesting that a Brit should be the one to take this approach; his first contact with the object of his desire was an attempt to instill in her a feeling of inferiority.

I had become that most dangerous of propositions: a beautiful girl with the mind of a man. Actress and agent in one. Pimp and ho. And as such, I conformed effortlessly to men's stereotype of women: *All women are basically sluts who barter their bodies to get what they want.*

No wonder I met with such universal approval. One guy sent email after email after email. What did he think? That I hadn't received the others? That he'd catch me at a weak moment and I'd let him fuck me? Far from being flattering, so many uninvited emails were just pathetic. *The book is about an older guy who becomes obsessed with a young photographer's assistant (you might pick up some tips). Okay, I'll get it today. I need some new fiction.* He was already taking part in some. Another guy wrote three weeks after he'd bought the book. *I'm still interested in getting to know you. What do I have to do?* He was a sad-looking little guy. Bald, of course. Probably wanking off over pictures of my lovely girlfriend's ass. Of course he wanted to fuck her. So did I. He'd have to get in line. One guy was on the right track with *Call me paranoid, but are you the author?* I thought he was onto me until he began to unspool a vertiginous scenario in which he suggested Francoise was the French girlfriend mentioned at the end of the book and that she had written it anonymously, pretending to be the oxygen thief. *so you think I wrote the book? I wish* Two days later he sent Francoise a glowing review. I think he enjoyed it all the more for having been introduced to it in such an unusual way.

It certainly helped that the book talked about sex, dating, and booze. Hardly a difficult sell for most men. In fact, I was very often thanked for recommending it, even though they knew they would never get in my pants. A pretty girl hinting that a guy should buy something is seen as normal. The guy expects the girl to make him pay for something. To prove he's a good provider. He is expected to pay, and often wants to. It's understood that a woman requires a token gift in return for her company. Tickets to the opera, or a concert, or a movie, cab fares, dinner, flowers. All she is expected to do in return is look fabulous, nod a lot, and smile as if she's enjoying herself.

These were professional, well-spoken, highly cultured men, occupying some of New York's top positions in the arts and media. They were what we referred to in advertising as opinion formers. They were even more sought after than the target audience, because these were the people the target audience looked to when they wanted to know what was cool.

You can feed a dog organic vegetables and over time he'll adapt, but put a steak in front of him and his true nature will show. These cosmopolitan journalists, architects, web producers, lawyers, copywriters, designers, artists, and entrepreneurs were salivating at the prospect of a superior piece of French ass. But even though the photos plainly showed a half-naked girl with a beautiful body, they had learned through years of conditioning that they needed to feign indifference to her sexuality and compliment her photographic technique instead. What would a photographer's assistant want to hear? She'd obviously want to hear how well her photos were composed. They were supremely confident they could dupe this inexperienced little fawn. At only twenty-three, she was obviously confused about how much flesh she should show. She was probably some rich French guy's daughter who had no idea how to behave.

Someone was going to fuck her, so why not be that guy?

A certain senior copywriter and media spokesperson (my Google search showed he was widely quoted), wanted to be that guy. A sixty-two-year-old man, sniffing around the beautiful ass of my thirty-six-year-old girlfriend, posing as a twenty-three-year-old French girl. And yes, he was married, with three kids. Well, so what? He was a media guru, wasn't he? He'd made it to the top, hadn't he? This was Manhattan, wasn't it?

In reality, we were just two old ad guys trading copy.

Meanwhile, I'd look at Marian when she turned up to meet me and I'd have to pinch myself. It was as if I was going out with a model. A moody model. She was even more beautiful now that I was losing her. I couldn't tell whether we were running on fumes or if this was the lull before re-igniting our relationship. In reality, I think we were both just too lazy to stop seeing each other. I was the one guy among hundreds lucky enough to be with her, but she could hardly bear it when I touched her. She visibly flinched before I even made contact. I had caused this in her? She said it was a relief to talk to her doctor about a neck ache because at least he didn't roll his eyes waiting for her to finish.

This was a dig at me, and I blushed in acknowledgment.

But I had never really been able to follow her thread when she spoke because she jumped around from point to point without warning, and when I asked for clarification she became irritated, because in her mind she had already supplied this information, and if I was asking such a question, it meant I hadn't listened the first time around, and if I hadn't been listening then, it had to mean I didn't care about her, and if I didn't care about her, why was I trying to touch her?

Yeah, I know.

I decided to pretend harder. But pretend to be what? I couldn't trust my perception anymore. Did I want to stay with her only because she was such a great sales tool, or did I still love her for who she was before all that happened? Would she leave me in disgust as soon as she realized what I was doing? I couldn't even trust the enthusiastic responses to the book, emanating as they did from libidinous men who would say anything to get into the pants of the girl who had made the recommendation. The only irrefutable truth was the sales.

And yeah, they were plentiful.

I kept two pages open on my computer screen: one showing Francoise's profile, with its constant supply of eager supplicants, and another page showing the corresponding book orders on Amazon.

The main profile picture of Marian standing in my kitchen wearing a T-shirt and knee socks was like something by the French photographer Guy Bourdin, so I claimed it was a self-portrait paying homage to him. My book was now inseparably associated with two of France's most enduring style icons, Jane Birkin and Guy Bourdin.

And all three would be googled accordingly.

In the meantime, being with Marian was becoming impossible. There were too many subjects that couldn't be talked about. The silences grew longer and longer until they overlapped. We lied to each other by omission. The strange thing is that I got the impression we could have gone on like this for years. After all, I didn't want anyone else. To me she was perfect. Yes, of course, I saw attractive women everywhere, but compared to Marian they were just unknown accumulations of organs and limbs. They would never represent the bittersweet, unknowable concoction that only she possessed. She was exquisite confusion. Being touched by her was a triumphant, luxurious sensation. It was so flattering that she should even want to make me feel pleasure that somehow my guilt dissolved into gratitude under her touch. And there was that bottomless lust I felt for her, a spiritual longing that no mere physical exchange could ever extinguish.

But even as the sales soared and the reviews enthused, I knew we had to make a clean break of it. No contact. It was the only way. We'd be friends, yes, of course, but just not yet. It was too soon for that. Just making the decision felt like a mental siege had been lifted. For two days the relief was euphoric, until suddenly an entire civilization seemed to burn down inside me.

Devastation.

In her cavernous absence I replayed and blinked away the awful moment she confronted me about the datemedot com message on her computer. This would be my punishment. As the weeks turned into months, we never got the chance to discuss anything because we were too busy, I suppose, recovering from each other. In fact, this book is the closest I've come to letting her know what I actually thought and why.

The previous year, when things were still good, we'd had a lovely day wandering around Williamsburg. It was one of those rare weekends when her roommate visited her parents and we had the entire apartment to ourselves. We had just had fabulous sex, or least I had, and Marian looked so effortlessly beautiful it seemed like we had stepped onto a hundred-acre set of a commercial for jeans or sneakers or maybe even a romantic comedy with an edge. The Williamsburg Bridge poked into every picture I took of her, and we laughed knowingly at the very idea that even here, so deep behind the Irony Curtain, it was possible to be "in love."

I mentioned in passing that I played piano, that I had taught myself to play on a crappy old upright we had at home in Ireland. The fact that she thought I was joking seemed to indicate she hoped it was true. We entered a music store but found there was a sign saying NO LIVE MUSIC, which still seems fucking stupid to me today, but they probably had so many people jamming in there they had to ban it. With great ceremony I held a pair of head-phones apart and invited her to step into them. Arranging them just so like a tiara over her bowed head, I plugged them into a digital piano, and as we stood there side by side I began to play. All I could hear were the keys fumbling and clicking as my fingers stumbled and drummed across them. I had no way of knowing if she was enjoying what she heard or if, indeed, she could hear anything at all, but I kept play-ing anyway.

Wary of missing a key, I darted a look at her. The effect on her face was magical. Her eyes had filled with wonder, and her smile radiated joy. All the self-consciousness had peeled away to reveal an innocence so pure it made me want to dance. I felt like I had at last found a way to communicate with her. As I sit here typing, these same fingers fumbling over similar keys, I am reminded of that day.

I'd like to speak to the person who put this profile together. This was from a forty-five-year-old entrepreneur who had posted pictures of himself relaxing on what looked like a yacht in what could have been the Mediterranean.

He was onto me.

Some guys might be very pissed off if they knew that their romantic attentions were in fact being pitched not at a hot French twenty-three-year-old with an ass to match but at a bald middle-aged Mick in his underpants. Actually, I didn't even wear underpants most of the time.

I might be overthinking this, but I have some questions.

You're the French girlfriend?
You are the French girlfriend mentioned at the end of the book, and you're helping the author sell his book. In that case, you would be using datemedotcom as a social media platform to generate an audience, which is really impressive, and I'm sure it's working very well. You certainly got me. I would love to hear from you both and, if possible, set up a time to meet.

You're a fan of the book?
You really are who you say you are: Francoise, a stunningly beautiful and sexy photographer who happens to

be a fan of this book. In that case, I should tell you I am not like the author. Not at all. I've had different issues in my life that I would be happy to talk about over dinner. I would love to hear from you, and I would very much like to meet you.

You (Francoise) wrote the book?
If that's the case, you are a talent of unmitigated genius. I have worked with marketers for decades, and your accounts are very familiar to me. My career parallels the novel's time frame, and it's quite possible we've met before. I thank you for exposing me to the book and for this exchange. I would love to have you sign my copy of the book.

Franciose is the creation of the anonymous author?
Genius! I'm already hugely impressed with the book, but creating this inviting atmosphere around it to bring people into it—fantastic! The experience of engaging with you in this way via this character is spectacular. With the utmost respect, and, if necessary, discretion, I would love to shake your hand and see if we might work together.

I hadn't thought about using this technique for anything other than selling my own book, but it suddenly occurred to me that in the same way an ad agency can advertise any product as long as the approach is well conceived, so could I, with this more subtle method of covertising, sell anything to anyone. Would it work? You tell me.

THE END

wow . . . devoured the book in two big, greedy gulps. it's dark, smooth, and jagged edged . . . like a fresh piece of broken glass that you want to touch even though you know you shouldn't.

• • • •

francoise, just picked up the book this evening. looks like an easy read. I'll get back to you with my thoughts soon, so yeah, I guess I'm game, k

• • • •

listen, I would have written before but, uh, your profile says you're looking for a woman, *which sort of threw me off because now you're all flirting with me. I'm sooooo shy lately and totally caged up in my place working from home a lot. it's sort of pathetic. tell me how you are.*

• • • •

francoise . . . so, I'm also a big fan of films and sex. and I design books for a living, which makes me an automatic fan (speaking of which . . . I just tried to order diary of an oxygen thief and it says they're sold out!! . . . and I hate ordering things from Amazon). anyhow, I'm intrigued, how is your tuesday so far? best jimmi

• • • •

hello francoise . . . well I've been spending quite a bit of time on google this morning looking up guy bourdin and that book you mentioned, as, no I haven't read it and hadn't even heard

of it. I see what you mean though, looks pretty heavy and intense (alcoholism, abuse, photographers assistant etc). unfor-
tunately it appears to be out of stock, so I may need to do a bit
of digging around to get a copy.

• • • •

don't mind at all. I have not read the book. just googled it. seems
to be about a guy who's emotionally sadistic toward women. an
ad guy! (I'm a copywriter.) well, a british ad guy, that's different.
don't want to judge the book without having read it, but I probably would not identify with an emotionally selfish and reckless
character. then again, there are no angels on this earth. you sound
very interesting. what kind of writing/photography do you do?

• • • •

uhmmm . . . I'm a little confused. you sort of asked me the
same thing last week. did you get my response?

• • • •

francoise . . . no, I dont know that book, looked it up though
and it sounds sizzling. is it still anonymous, or did the author
come out? have you been in nyc long? where are you living?
you can email me for real if you like.
Olivier

• • • •

yeah, I'm game . . . just picked up the book this evening. looks
like an easy read. I'll get back to you with my thoughts soon.
hope you're well.

• • • • •

I will seek out the oxygen thief book at once, though it seems a difficult tome to locate. I do love a challenge. your guy bourdin tribute is striking. is your frying pan non-stick? it would be better placed in my firm hand, my other gripping the nape of your neck . . . are you a fan of baudelaire?

• • • • •

hi your profile is definitely intriguing but hard to see whether you have only one eye or not (then again one eye might be sexy ummm). vous etes francaise? je suis quebecois mais d'origine italienne allors je parle francais comme une vache espagnole. let's talk oh mysterious stranger.

• • • •

hey I'm studying to be a pilates instructor and was thinking if you needed to practice your photography it would be cool to take some shots of me doing my stretches.

• • • •

how come you didn't answer any of my emails if you're going to hotlist me again? I don't mind playing around on here but it's more fun if there is a dialogue.

• • • •

francoise . . . glad you still have all your limbs. not that paraplegics can't be sexy too.

• • • •

taking any good portraits these days? intense book, do you really recommend that?

• • • •

you're not very good at this, are you . . . ? I see that you're looking for a girl, not a guy. so, what's the attraction . . . ? just a playmate/friend? someone to borrow cool lenses from? (you'd have to have a canon.) someone to make your current girlfriend jealous? what's the story . . . ? might I say that your pictures are amazing and I bet you are too? what's your name? I'm allan . . . when are you free? today. lunch! 1pm . . . my place?

• • • •

you got "woman" in your "looking for" section but your copy says you're looking for a guy. I'm above your age range but you "looked" so I thought I'd wave and just point out the gender issue. nice pictures.

• • • •

now that you posted pictures, I think I can fairly speak for all lesbians when I say that they'd be more than happy to have you playing on their team, if you ever chose to. I'll check out that book you mentioned.

• • • •

Eff . . . funny you should mention that book—someone I met at a party recently suggested I read it. I'm going to look for it today and will let you know my reactions. then you can tell me what it says about me. it will be a good exercise for both of us.

• • • •

hi there miss francoise, did you hotlist me by accident? (aged 60)

• • • •

hi beautifullylit, thanks for adding me to your hotlist. and thanks for recommending the book. it looks very interesting. you're smashingly cute, though I wish your face were . . . um . . . beautifully lit rather than semi-obscured. is being a professional portrait photographer as cool as it sounds? hope you're having a fun weekend.

• • • •

the minimalist profile. it leaves more to one's imagination, a lost art really. you've clearly mastered the art of seduction through photos as well. I have no idea what you look like and my mind will wander endlessly until I do. nicely done, au bientot

• • • •

how's it going? I'm also a fan of art, culture, and sex although not necessarily in that order and have kind of made a career out of two of the three. have you seen anything cool recently? your photos are very intriguing. do you have more?
look forward to hearing more about you.

• • • •

yes I read it. . . . enjoyed it . . . in about a day and a half. liked the nyc parts I recognized, and really felt for the guy when he just wanted her to say "yeah, let's get lunch" but "no, sorry, busy, parents, blah . . ." ouch. among other excruciating parts. he certainly did get his. a lot of wincing on my part. good tour of the inside of his head . . .

For more information about alcoholism and/or sex addiction, go to aa.org and/or slaafws.org.